# The Wide Boy$

Julian Moss

Notes from the main character – Buster Wide….

Any similarity to persons livin' or brown bread (dead) is coincidental, but if you think any of these characters sound a bit like you, or if you think you've done some of them silly things what is written in 'ere – I wouldn't admit to it.

Published by Camilian Publishing, Los Angeles, California

www.camilianpublishing.com

www.julianmoss.com

ISBN: 1941265006
ISBN-13: 978-1-941265-00-0

This book is dedicated to my fabulous parents; Daphne and Graham Moss.

Thank you for life and everything that comes with it.

Long may you live – just don't spend all the inheritance, as I doubt this book will add much to my pension.

I wish to thank:

Camille Alexander for the cover design, your love , encouragement and companionship.

To Alison Manheim for her proofreading

To Beth Wimmer for her keen eyes

And to you, the reader, for braving the words of a new author.

# CONTENTS

The names, characters and events portrayed in this book are based entirely on bulls**t.

# CHAPTER 1

It is evening and the cicadas are chirping loudly, interspersed with the deep croak of an African bullfrog. Broad rubber-plant leaves overlap each other in a scramble for light. The open flowers of orchids tempt non-existent insects, and an array of small cacti share the soil with unusual neighbors: basil and rosemary. Thyme has no place here. A white bunny rabbit hops a few feet and sniffs the backside of a tortoise munching on a lettuce leaf atop an Afghan rug. A parrot sits on a branch and surveys his strange surroundings.

The living room of Aurora's apartment is one of a tropical landscape antithetical to the reality of suburban Calabasas, a town thirty miles northwest of downtown Los Angeles. In amongst the concrete jungle of upscale track housing is Aurora's oasis of a faux Amazonian climate, aided by air conditioning and electricity. The noises of the rain forest emanate from a relaxation soundtrack that is playing through an iPod system.

Shelves are packed with books on self-help, spiritualism, feng shui, personal growth, organic food, yoga, colon cleansing, alternative energy as well as a Barbara Cartland novel or two. Against the wall, near the humidifier and the acupuncture chart, is a yoga mat with little pieces missing at the bottom, bitten away by the inquisitive tortoise. Aromatic candles burning scents of an English garden confuse the sights with the senses, but add a romantic luminescence to the main room.

Eagerly awaiting their dinner are Aurora's guests, sitting on hard bench seats at the rectangular oak table. The most vocal of the four is Buster, a Cockney from London's East End, with a devil-may-care attitude towards life and its laws.

"I tell you, Rachel, you could do worse than listen to my brother and me about what's really important in life," says the

1

rugged-looking Englishman with a lifetime of street smarts crammed into his thirty-six earthly ones. He is pure working-class, as is his brother, Dwayne, also seated at the table. "Because life is simply what you make it. And playin' by the rules ain't necessarily the right way, neither."

"That's right, young lady," adds Dwayne, a couple of years younger than his brother, two inches shorter and dimmer than a 40-watt light bulb. Buster may not be an Einstein, but Dwayne makes an amoeba appear capable of understanding the principals of nuclear fusion. He looks up from working on a rudimentary crossword puzzle. "Rules is what the big man wants you to follow, because the big man don't want you to become a big man like him, who didn't follow the rules in the first place in order to become the big man." His voice is raspy, like that of a long-time smoker, although neither brother smokes.

Rachel, the object of their worldly wisdom, is only nine years of age. She is not just bright, but is rumored to have been born clutching a PhD. She sits at the table next to Dwayne and opposite Buster and her California-born mother, Tiffany.

"Well, I'm going to Harvard to study quantum mechanics and string theory," she says confidently.

Buster smiles indulgently.

"Learnin' about car engines and textiles is all fine and dandy, but street smarts is what really gets you through life. Just look at me," he says, leaning back and puffing his chest out immodestly, "the apothecary of success."

"Epitome," says Rachel.

"I don't pity anyone," says Buster. "If you can't handle the heat, get out of the fryer."

"Fire!" corrects Rachel.

"Where?" Buster and Dwayne look around, then back to Rachel.

In the adjacent kitchen, Aurora is listening to the conversation while preparing the dinner of raw food for her carnivorous guests. She is a lithe woman in her early thirties, vegan thin and Polar bear pale. Large, dark eyes make her gaunt face appear smaller, and her lack of makeup does not detract from her natural good looks. She is a product of California, where the ethereal, spiritual and self-enlightened way-of-life, with all its narcissism, is alive and flourishing. She tosses a salad in a large ceramic bowl and begins to dish it out.

"Anyway," resumes Buster in his deep Cockney voice. "Life is pretty pointless and then you die. But on the way, there are a few bright spots to keep ya goin'." He looks adoringly at Tiffany sitting next to him. "Like the love of a good woman."

"And the love of a good man," replies Tiffany, a kind-hearted woman who is three years older than her sister, Aurora. She has a fuller body and could be as attractive if she made the effort, but she is more of a humanist than a narcissist. She looks up at Buster as if he is the centre of her universe.

"Of course, romance isn't without its ups and downs, broken hearts and reneged prenuptial contracts. I remember the advice my mother once gave to me. She said 'Son, it's better to have loved and lost, than to spend your whole life wanking!'"

Buster reaches for Tiffany's hand. They share a loving look.

"Awww," says Tiffany, looking coyly up at her man.

"Street smarts, eh, Buster?" inquires Aurora, as she walks to the table with three plates of a green, leafy salad. She flicks her wavy, center-parted auburn hair over her shoulder so that it does not land in the food. Placing the plates in front of Buster, Rachel and Tiffany she says, "Is that why you and Dwayne left England for Los Angeles?"

"No, no. It was because you don't believe in the Royal family, wasn't it?" interjects Tiffany, squeezing Buster's hand supportively. "Something about not wanting to be detained at Her Majesty's pleasure."

"Er, yeah, somethin' like that," says Buster, glancing sheepishly at his brother, both recognizing the euphemism for "going to prison."

"Don't listen to him, Rachel. If your mother's boyfriend is such a street-smart businessman, how come your mom's paying all the rent?" She walks back to the kitchen.

"That's not nice,....*Janet*!" snaps Buster, tight-lipped, emphasizing her true name. There is no love lost between the two.

"My name's Aurora, thank you." Her external beauty camouflages the hard, alpha-female businesswoman within. She returns with two more plates and her nose in the air. "Janet's my earthly name, Aurora's what the universe gave me." She puts the plates down in front of Dwayne and herself, then sits at the table.

"Well, *Aurora,* Dwayne and I are goin' through a transitional time right now, re-adjustin' our goals in life and seekin' new ventures that will bring us prosperity," says Buster.

"You'd have found prosperity if you just believed in *The Shhh* like Dwayne does."

"Not that bloody thing again," groans Buster, sitting back in his chair.

"It manifested all this," says Aurora, arms outstretched. With her loose fitting, tie-dyed caftan dress, nobody is aware of her forest-like armpit hair, and while the room may appear Brazilian, parts of her body certainly do not.

"It's just a way of makin' money off weak-minded people," retorts Buster. He freezes in thought and mutters, "Sounds like the American dream, actually."

Rachel looks confused.

"What's *The Shhh*?" she asks.

"It's a self-help DVD about positive imagery and visualizin' abundance," affirms Dwayne verbatim, looking over his crossword puzzle book at her.

"Dwayne found abundance when he found me," says Aurora, proudly. "Didn't you?"

"Yes, dear."

"Sit up, Dwayne. Use the Alexander technique," nags Aurora.

"Yes, dear."

Buster stares at his plate of salad.

"Did you just mow the lawn? Where's the meat?"

"Around the bones of the animals in the fields, where nature intended." Aurora pours herself a glass of water. "This is an organic, raw vegan meal and healthy for your colon. Keeps you regular and prevents disease. Isn't that right, Dwayne?"

"Yes, dear," replies Dwayne. "Although, I've eaten so much greenery in the last year that when I go outside I notice I start bendin' towards the sun!" Dwayne nudges Rachel who laughs along with everyone, except Aurora.

"But your colon is thanking you," she whips.

"Yeah, I've heard it," mutters Buster.

"Put your crossword away, Dwayne, so we can say a blessing," says Aurora.

Rachel glances at Dwayne's crossword puzzle before he closes
it.

"That one's wrong."

"Which one?"

"Seven down. A four-letter word, another name for a woman.
Last three letters U.N.T." The adults look to each other with
concern. "That should be aunt, A.U.N.T."

"Oh." Dwayne corrects his mistake then places the book on the
floor.

"Prayer time," insists Aurora. Buster sighs deeply, but Tiffany
gives him a pleading look, so he acquiesces. The hostess reaches
out her hands for the others to hold in a prayer ring. Reluctantly,
they hold each other's hands around the table. "Earth, we thank
you for your abundance, for providing us with this glorious
nutrition to keep us healthy, regular and polyp-free. And I want to
apologize on behalf of the human race for slaughtering your
innocent animals, for choking you with our pollution and for
dumping carcinogens into the sea. And God, can you come up with
a cure for all the stupid people? Thanks." She breaks the prayer
ring and smiles at everyone. "Go ahead. Enjoy." Aurora starts to
eat with relish.

Dwayne begins, but Buster just pokes at his food with his fork.

"Oh, Buster, nearly forgot. I got the architect's plans for the
pub back today," says Dwayne, stabbing at his salad.

"Great. I'll look at them later."

"Architect plans?" echoes Aurora curiously. "I didn't think you
had the money to pay for an architect."

"We don't," says Dwayne. "I got a student at USC to do them
for us for free." He smiles then winks at Aurora. "That's the power
of positive thinkin'."

"He gets credits for college, we get our plans for free," adds
Buster, forking at the mass of greenery.

"How are you going to build it? You don't have *any* money,
not a red cent. And seeing as how you don't believe in *The Shhh*
and the law of attraction, you're not likely to either," says Aurora.
"Your brother's more likely to get the cash than you. Believing in
*The Shhh* he can visualize the money."

"Oh, I can visualize it," Buster assures her. "Just can't get me
bleedin' hands on it."

5

"How much do you need again?" asks Tiffany, grazing on her salad.

"Three quarters of a million."

"And how much do you have now?" asks Aurora.

"About...a hundred," says Dwayne with his mouth full.

"Grand?" asks Tiffany, impressed.

"No, dollars," says Dwayne.

"Oh, good. At least you'll have toilet paper," replies Aurora. "What are you doing about the rest of it? You know, like buying an actual piece of land to build on?"

"We know this guy from the gym, called Michael," adds Dwayne. "He's in real estate and knows a farmer that's lettin' a slice of land go for a song."

"What song's that – *Jailhouse Rock*?" asks Aurora. "Sounds illegal to me."

"No, luv," chimes in Dwayne. "It's on the up and up."

"Really? Well, if Buster doesn't make some money soon, he'll end up in one of those homeless shelters where Tiffany works," says Aurora.

"There're worse places to be," says Buster, braving a mouthful of the salad.

"Like England?"

Aurora and Buster share a look of mutual disdain. Aurora looks to her sister.

"Not still bringing your work home, are you?" she asks.

"Do you know that there are barely fifteen-hundred beds for sixty thousand homeless in L.A. County?"

"Well, if they all had beds, they wouldn't be called homeless would they?" says Aurora with tactless logic.

"Give it a rest. Tiffany's a saint. And I don't mind the odd homeless person at the apartment every now and then," says Buster. "Except for the smell sometimes."

"They get used to us," quips Rachel, as she eats voraciously.

"I just don't think it's healthy to leave those kinds of people alone with Rachel."

"Don't worry, Aunt Aurora," says Rachel. "I won't hurt them."

"We're all just tryin' to get ahead in this world, that's all," says Buster.

"How can you be getting ahead when your idea of success is

*not* winning the lottery?" asks Aurora, shaking her head in disbelief. "Are you still *not* playing?"

"Of course. I look at it this way," says Buster, putting down his fork, as if he needs hand gestures to make his point. "There is a one in a hundred and fifty million chance of winnin' the lotto. I have the same numbers that I don't play each week: three, seven, sixteen, forty-four, forty-five and the mega number nine. At five bucks a go, twice a week, I haven't won the jackpot in over four hundred attempts in the last four years. That's almost two thousand bucks I haven't wasted. I look at that as a success." He winks at Rachel, picks up his fork and continues to eat.

"You could have won fifty-four bucks once," corrects Dwayne.

"Yeah, okay."

"Then a couple of times you would have won nine bucks."

"Okay, okay. I think I might have inadvertently won a hundred bucks had I actually played, but that means I'm still one-thousand-nine-hundred bucks ahead by not playin'."

Tiffany pats his hand lovingly.

"I'm so proud of you."

Buster smiles back at her, then sourly at Aurora.

"You're a fine one to talk about Tiffany and her work. At least she's got a proper job, helpin' people."

"I help people."

"You hustle people as a self-imposed spiritual guru, selling dreams and hope to the lost and lonely. Trust me, I know a con-artist when I see one."

"Oh, I'm sure you do." Aurora's eyes narrow. "I live what I preach." She looks around the room, then at Dwayne. "Dwayne, remind your brother why we don't have a television."

"Rots the brain," he says, unconvincingly.

"No newspapers?" she continues.

"Means killin' trees."

"No car?"

"Pollutes the air."

"Internet?"

"Porn."

"But you've got an iPad, an iPhone, and a web site," says Buster, smugly. "Bit hypocritical, ain't it?"

"I'm forced to use those by society's demands in order to keep my business going."

Buster shakes his head, then picks up a small cellophane packet and tears it open, squeezing the wine-soaked sponge inside it into a glass.

"I bet this pub is just another one of your hair-brained schemes, like your 'wine in a sponge' idea?" smirks Aurora.

"I don't know why this didn't catch on. We've got wine in a bottle, wine in a box. I thought wine in a sponge was just obvious. You spill some, sponge it up and squeeze again. Don't waste a drop." He looks bemused at it. "Still got five thousand left." His face lights up with a bright idea. "I know, I could donate them to the homeless shelters."

"Um, not a good idea," replies Tiffany.

"Buster, you really need to watch *The Shhh*. It'll give you the tools to visualize abundance and attract financial security," says Aurora. "Plus, if you get into my downstream, you can create your own multi-level marketing web and make money that way."

"There's more to success than just visualizin' it and thinkin' that it's goin' to happen. There is such a thing as action. And action is what we're takin'."

"Yeah, we're goin' to see Michael about the property tomorrow," chimes in Dwayne.

"What's the point if you don't have the money for a deposit? The banks aren't going to give you two a mortgage without a deposit or a job."

Rachel stares at her plate.

"My food moved!" she says.

Everyone ignores her.

"Well, dear," says Dwayne looking ingratiatingly at Aurora. "I'm thinkin' positive thoughts. I've visualized the money. Where it comes from I don't know, but that's part of *The Shhh*, right?"

"Visualize it? Ha! Like when you visualized abundance by gettin' into photography?" He looks at Rachel and smirks. "Most people photograph weddings or families or kids. But d'you know what hitherto untapped market my brother here decided to photograph?" She shakes her head. Dwayne looks embarrassed. "Funerals!"

"Funerals?" echoes Rachel in disbelief.

Buster leans back in his chair, taking the moment to chuckle at his brother.

"Yeah, you should've seen him. I went along to hold the reflector thingy. We was all suited up, we was, lookin' like the dog's bollocks, waitin' for the vicar guy to finish what he was sayin' around the grave, you know, like they do. Well, anyway, the vicar finishes and walks away, and before anyone could leave, Dwayne here gathers them all up around the grave site and says things like 'Come on then, group up. Bunch together around Grandma.' Well, they did of course, all in black, standin' around the hole and the mound of dirt, when clever Dick here starts givin' it all that," says Buster, making the universal sign of talking by opening and closing his fingers and thumb. "So, then he says somethin' like 'Come on, less of the gloomy. Let's have ya smilin' into the camera. Nice one for the obituary column. Say cheese!'" Buster giggles. "Well, stone the crows, if they ain't all gettin' into it and posin' along. There was this blonde bird there, tasty sort she was, hammin' it up to the camera. So, Dwayne here is eggin' her on sayin', 'That's it. Keep it comin' luv. You've got more style than Vidal Sassoon, baby, more curves than British Rail.' Next thing I know is that blondie's boyfriend is startin' in on Dwayne thinkin' he was on the pull. Nearly clocked him one, he did. Funniest thing I've seen in ages, I tell ya." Buster laughs and combs his fingers though his mousy-blonde, side-parted hair.

Rachel laughs at the description. Dwayne looks embarrassed.

"At least it was legal," retorts Dwayne. "More than can be said for your Thanksgivin' sale scam at the department store."

"Well, let's not get into that." Buster's smile is instantly wiped from his face.

"So, this is what Buster does," begins Dwayne, now eager to even the score. He puts down his cutlery and looks at everyone in turn. "My big brother here pulls a fast one on a big department store here in L.A."

"Which one?" cuts in Aurora.

"Best if you don't know," replies Dwayne. "So, picture this. Good few years ago now and it's the day after Thanksgivin' and you've got half of America outside this department store waitin' to get in and grab the holiday bargains. Doors open, in flood the greedy buggers. One of them is our Buster here. Only difference is that he's brought his own till under his long coat."

"What's a till?" asks Rachel.

"Er, cash register, I think you Yanks call 'em," answers Dwayne. "Anyway, he's been scopin' out the store for ages, seein' how the employees are dressed and what their badges looked like. So, come the day, in all the madness, Buster quickly strips down to his fake uniform and props the till up on an empty counter and starts takin' sales. Cash only, of course."

"Where there's a till there's a way," says Buster proudly, raising his glass of wine in a sponge, and drinking.

"I was his lookout in the store. Anyway, right near the end of the day some manager got suspicious. Before he called security, I signaled to Buster. You should have seen him grab the takings and leg it," laughs Dwayne.

"Made a killin' though, didn't I?"

"What did you do with the money?" asks Aurora.

"Dunno, really. Spent it on this and that."

"If you'd put it into a mutual fund and diversified your interest, you could have netted six to eight percent pre-tax profit," says Rachel. "You might have had enough to leverage a bank loan for the pub you want to buy."

The four adults stare at Rachel.

"Well, yeah, obviously," says Buster, feeling stupid.

"Goes without sayin', really," echoes Dwayne.

"Anyway, those dodgy days are behind me. Now I got a good woman." He looks from Tiffany to Rachel. "Make that *two* good women to look after. The pub is our retirement present."

"Retire from what? By your own admission, you haven't done an honest day's work in your entire life," rebukes Aurora.

"Not so. We're doin' the eBay thing."

"Like that's moral? You go round picking up free stuff and giveaways on sites like Craigslist, then sell them on eBay?" says Aurora, incredulously.

"Great profit margin," says Buster.

"But your place is packed *full* of that junk. Every room is so stuffed that you can't even have people like me over for dinner," complains Aurora.

"That's a cryin' shame," mutters Buster as he takes another sip of wine.

"It's just temporary," says Tiffany. "Until we get ahead."

"You would be ahead if you stopped giving what little money you earn back to the homeless, sis," says Aurora.

"They need all the help they can get," says Tiffany.

Aurora looks to Buster and Tiffany.

"You *both* need to come to one of my life coaching classes. I can show you how to live a transformed life worth living."

"Eighty bucks an hour to tell people how to live their lives? You should call yourself Dick Turpin, 'cause that's highway robbery."

Buster lifts up his fork and discovers a snail on it. Everyone stares in horror.

"Finally, some protein!"

Just over five miles northeast of Calabasas, on the other side of the 101 freeway, is a place called West Hills, brilliantly named by someone who came upon them from the east. It is a residential area comprising of bungalows and detached houses with a sprinkling of apartment complexes and convenience stores.

In one such bungalow live two men in their 20's who are friends but polar opposites of each other in looks and demeanor. Greg is tall and skinny, with a thick mop of dark hair that has a mind of its own. Which is good, because Greg does not. His chest seems to sink inwards like a deflated soufflé. Like a child wearing his father's clothes, Greg is swallowed up in a shirt made for a man seventy pounds heavier. His neck rattles around the shirt collar like a tortoise in a shell. His voice is deep, but his intellect not so much.

Carl, on the other hand, is foot shorter with a round, shaved head with protruding ears and slightly bulging eyes. On first seeing Carl, people often think that they have seen him before, as he resembles the human version of Dopey from "Snow White and the Seven Dwarfs". The two have been friends since school, both bullied for their physical differences and both ignored by women for similar reasons.

Greg stands in front of a full-length mirror.

"Wadda ya think? This one or this one?" he asks, holding up a long, blue dress and a shorter red one to his six feet three inches stick insect of a body.

"Errrr…the red one." Carl holds a yellow dress to his chest. They consider their reflections in the mirror by the door in the

11

living room.

"Really? I thought the blue dress made me look fuller, you know, less skinny."

"Wear the blue one then. What do I care?" Carl is the more decisive of the two. He looks between Greg's blue dress to the yellow one he is holding. "Hang on. We can't both wear primary colors."

"Good point. I'll wear the red one."

"Right." Carl picks up a couple of wigs from the sofa and hands one to Greg. "You wanna be blonde or brunette?"

"Blonde," says Greg. "I hear they have more fun."

"At your height, they'd probably have altitude sickness."

Carl hands him a wig. They both put them on and look at their reflections. Without saying a word, they simultaneously swap wigs and put them on. Carl nods with satisfaction, content to be a blonde.

"I can't believe we're actually doing this," says Greg, giggling like a schoolgirl.

"It'll change our lives forever."

Back in Aurora's open plan, faux equatorial kitchen, Dwayne stands at the sink, cleaning dishes with acidic water, the bi-product of her alkaline water machine. He uses Aurora's organic soap, made from the diaphragms of fifteen thousand mentally handicapped beetles, who all died of natural causes – or so she was told by the head of the multi-level marketing firm that sold them to her. Dwayne washes up by the light of nearly exhausted candles.

Aurora remains in the living room, stroking the leaves of a rubber plant.

"I thought that went quite well," she remarks, holding a leaf to her cheek and smiling. "Good night, plant. Thank you for your oxygen today." She then calls out to Dwayne at the sink. "I'm so glad that you've transformed your life to one of health and vitality."

With his back to her, Dwayne secretly pulls a piece of beef jerky from his pocket and bites into it, chewing quickly, then placing it back in his pocket.

"Uh-huh."

"I worry for young Rachel, though. I'm not convinced that

Buster is the right role model for her." Aurora tickles the parrot. "After all, he's not her actual father. And children are so easily influenced."

Dwayne looks up, thoughtfully.

"Buster and I never had a father. My mum brought us up on her own. We didn't turn out so bad."

Aurora begins to blow out the candles.

"Except for your names. Buster Wide? Whatever possessed your mum to call him Buster? And what about you, Dwayne? Dwayne Wide? What was she thinking?"

"Could have been worse. When I was about five, my mum nearly married a man named Edward Pipe. I could have been Dwayne Pipe. Anyway, your real name's Janet Hogarth not Aurora Neptune." Dwayne resumes washing dishes.

"That was my name in retail. The Universe called me into its service and now I'm Aurora Neptune." She looks around the floor. "You haven't seen Flopsy, have you?"

Dwayne realizes that he has the rabbit in one hand and is cleaning a plate with him. He quickly places the bunny on the floor by his feet.

"No, no." He picks up the dishcloth to dry the dishes.

"Oh, well," says Aurora holding the last remaining candle as she walks towards the corridor that leads to the bedroom. "Thank you, Earth for a wonderful day." She stops, looks to Dwayne and her face changes to displeasure. "Dwayne! Don't use the dishcloth. Let them dry naturally. Dishcloths spread germs." Dwayne puts the cloth down and looks around as Aurora walks out of the room, leaving him in the darkness by the sink. "Bed!" she commands.

"Yes, dear."

Dwayne quickly takes a dishcloth and, in defiance, aggressively wipes a plate before tossing the dishcloth to one side. He takes another bite of the beef jerky and chews with relish.

In between West Hills and Calabasas is a place called Hidden Hills. The hills are quite evident to the naked eye, so one can only surmise that irony took a significant part in its naming. Even in this quiet, up-market residential part of California, where backyard swimming pools are as common as puddles in England, there are still some average apartment buildings occupied by equally average people.

The apartment where Tiffany, Rachel and Buster live is in one such complex. It is a nice-sized two bedroom place, save the clutter of free furniture, golf clubs, clothing, fans, pots, kitchenware, computer monitors, old LPs and breast pumps gathered on Craigslist to be sold on eBay.

The master bedroom is the least cluttered. In bed, Buster sits up and makes notes on a pad of paper, while Tiffany climbs over the mess to get in next to him.

"Perhaps there's something to this positive thinking stuff like in *The Shhh* Aurora keeps talking about," she says, as she slips under the sheets.

"Mumbo jumbo, that's all. Trouble with Americans is that they'll believe any old crap that is put in front of them if they think it will make them richer. They're so gullible." He smiles approvingly. "I like that."

"But look at Aurora. She has a real job with a nice big apartment with nice things."

"She's a life coach, whatever that is. Sellin' the bleedin' obvious at eighty bucks an hour!" He looks up and thinks, tapping the pen to his lip. "Hmm. Maybe there's somethin' in this life coach thing after all."

"It's just that I would like to get the living room back so I could have people over once in a while," says Tiffany, snuggling down into bed.

"Well, that's what I'm workin' on, dear, with this pub deal. I really feel that this is it, the big one."

"But how are you going to pay for it?"

"Dunno right now."

"Would you rather I didn't give so much back to the homeless?"

"Na. I see it as an insurance policy in case we ever end up on the streets." He puts down the pad and pen then looks lovingly at Tiffany. "Don't you worry about the money. I'm like a cat, I am."

"What, you sleep all day?"

"No. I always land on my feet."

"Oh."

"It's alright, Tiff. I'll find a way. I always do." He hugs her and kisses the top of her head. "You mean the world to me and I want to buy it for you and that wonderful rug-rat of yours."

They kiss passionately.

"I love you, Buster Wide."

"Love you, too. Now let's get some kip." They snuggle down. Buster claps his hands. One set of lights turns off, as another set turns on. "Rachel, would you?"

Cocooned in her sleeping bag on the floor at the foot of the bed, Rachel reaches over and turns off the sound-sensitive light.

# CHAPTER 2

The sun beats down on the arid California ground like an abusive teacher's ruler on a disruptive pupil's hand.

In a dusty, dirt layby on a busy highway leading out of Calabasas, Buster, overdressed in a cheap seventies-style suit and an open-collared polyester shirt, leans against his old Ford. The car, like Buster himself, appears flashy on the outside but is less impressive on the inside. With sunglasses on, his exposed British skin soaks up the rays, while his scheming mind works on how to turn the idea of a British pub into a reality. Passing cars sound like a very slow version of a Formula One race, interspersed with silence whenever a hybrid model glides by.

At the sound of an approaching bicycle, Buster looks up to see Dwayne pulling up to a stop on a girl's pink-colored bicycle. Breathless, Dwayne pulls off a pair of swimming goggles, leaving oval pressure marks round both eyes.

"Allo." He pockets the goggles and looks around. "Michael ain't here then?"

"Obviously."

Dwayne gets off the bicycle and props it up on its stand.

"You look swanky, all dressed up," he says.

"Got that meetin' afterwards, ain't I." He looks at Dwayne dressed in shorts, a T-shirt and sandals over socked feet, then at the bicycle. "You came all that way on that thing?"

"Aurora wants me to be more environmentally friendly. Says cars pollute the environment. I blame Ed Begley, Jr."

Buster seems annoyed.

"Tell her that the carbon dioxide emissions from cars are needed for the plants to breathe and produce oxygen for us. So, cars are actually beneficial to the environment."

"You know I don't have the dosh to buy my own car anyway,

so I have to use her bike for a while."

"You'll have the car of your dreams when this deal goes through and we got our little British pub goin.'" Buster glances at his wristwatch. "If he ever turns up."

"Is there a toilet round here?" Dwayne shifts from foot to foot. "I really need to go and drop the kids off at the pool."

"It's all that rabbit food she makes you eat," says Buster.

A slick Chevrolet pulls off the highway and into the turnout. It is black and the windows are tinted, so it is almost impossible to see inside. The car comes to a rest in a dramatic cloud of dust. Before the dust has settled, the driver's door opens and a tall man steps out, looking sharp in his suit and tie. He puts on sunglasses and walks over to Buster and Dwayne.

Even with sunglasses on, the man looks very much like the actor Michael Keaton: piercing eyes, high forehead and recognizable mouth.

"Morning boys," says Michael, for as irony would have it, he also shares the actor's first name.

"Mornin', Michael," greets Buster.

"I see you found the spot?"

"Yeah. Unusual place to meet, I must say," says Buster.

"Keeps you from gettin' hounded by the press, I guess." From Dwayne's ingratiating smile, it's clear he actually believes that this real estate agent is, in fact, Michael Keaton having fallen on hard times. In Dwayne's defense, Keaton hasn't been on anyone's A-list for many years. "Don't suppose you know if there's a toilet around here?"

Michael looks at him strangely.

"Er, no." He turns his attention to Buster. "So, where are we with all this pub stuff?"

"On track. We got the architect plans," answers Buster. "Is the owner still interested in sellin' the land?"

"More now than ever." Michael walks back to his car, opens the passenger-side door and removes some documents. "Take a look at these," he says as he hands them to Buster.

Back in Calabasas, where small dogs are carried rather than walked and transients are considered residents who are only making minimum wage, privileged life goes on as usual.

Just off the main road is a shopping center containing a Ron's Supermarket flanked by a few smaller shops, all of them facing a large parking lot.

The supermarket's manager, Scott Linus, sits in his office dressed in a suit. He leans back in his chair, feet up on the desk, and tosses tiny paper balls at a toy basketball hoop fixed to the back of the door.

Hearing a knock at the door, the early-forties manager quickly sits up, fastens his tie and picks up the phone.

"Yes, I think that should do," he says in his Texan drawl. He cups his hand on the receiver as if he has been interrupted mid-conversation. "Come in!"

The door opens, revealing the portly African-American customer service manager.

"Well, I want to see those monthly reports on my desk before the end of the day," Scott says into the phone. He motions for Lawanda to wait a moment. "I don't want excuses, just results," he says, milking his performance. "Hang on a sec," he tells his imaginary caller. Then he covers the receiver again. "Yes?"

"When you're not too busy, there are a couple of customers who want to see you regarding a complaint."

"Can't you handle it?"

"They insisted on seeing the manager."

"Alright." Scott removes his hand from the phone's mouthpiece. "I have to go now. Some of us are busy. Just make sure those figures get to me." He hangs up. "Show them in, would you, Lawanda?"

She steps out for a moment and Scott looks at his computer screen. Hearing the click of high-heeled shoes, he looks up just as two burly-looking women step into his office.

Buster's finger moves over the surveyor's map spread out across Michael's hot car hood.

"This patch, here?" he asks.

"Yes. Corner lot, right near the mall at the outskirts of town. Perfect location for a pub, I think."

"And it belongs to a farmer, you say?" Buster is not fully convinced.

"He's got loads of farm land up the 405 Freeway past Magic

Mountain and a couple of little plots around here. I think he was planning to build on them. This particular property goes all the way back to that area, so you've got space for a parking lot and everything," says Michael, indicating the spot on the map.

"Yeah, great." Dwayne claps his hands together in the hopes of moving the proceedings along faster than his bowels. He looks around and puffs his cheeks in desperation.

"I can get the owner to sell this plot of land for less than a third of the actual value," says Michael. "You could just buy it and flip it and make money."

Buster looks at him suspiciously.

"Then why don't *you* buy it and flip it?"

"I don't have that kind of money or I would."

"Why's he sellin' again, Michael?" asks Dwayne, emphasizing the broker's first name as if it somehow makes them seem more like friends rather than just business associates.

"Because he's old, and his family, who he hates, is just waiting for him to croak, so they can then fight over his land."

"Why not just leave it to someone else in his will then…like us?" suggests Buster.

"He's worried that his will could be challenged after he pops off. So he'd rather sock it to his family now and sell it for far less than it's worth, just to piss them off."

"Sounds like a man after my own heart," Buster says with a smirk.

"How much are we talkin' about?" asks Dwayne.

"Hundred and fifty grand. But it's worth almost triple that. So, if I can get you this deal you have to pay me the commission based on the true value. Otherwise, why am I doing this, eh?"

"I guess it ain't because you're autistic," says Buster.

"I think you mean altruistic," corrects Michael. "So, you interested?"

"Sure," replies Buster. "Wouldn't mind takin' a look at it before makin' a final decision, though."

"I can arrange that. How soon can you get the money?"

"Well, that's the problem..." starts Dwayne.

"Er, shortly, shortly," interjects Buster, quickly cutting off his brother. "We gotta get it out of where it's at first."

"Well, don't be long. I can give you 'til the end of the month,

19

then I'll have to sell it, as I don't think the old fart will last much past that."

"Yeah, alright." Buster appears somewhat dejected.

"Okay, I gotta go to another meeting." Michael rolls up the surveyor's map.

"Okay, bye." Dwayne makes a beeline for his bicycle, briefly leaving Michael and Buster alone.

Michael leans into Buster.

"Does he still think I'm the actor that played Batman?" whispers Michael. "You know, Michael Keaton?"

"Yeah."

Michael smiles and nods his head like a wobble-dog toy on the dashboard of a car.

"Cool. Gotta go. Bye." Michael gets into his car and drives off in a plume of dramatic dust, just as Dwayne pushes his bicycle up to Buster.

"Where are we goin' to come up with a hundred and fifty big ones before the end of the month?" he asks.

"Dunno. That's only a couple of weeks away," says Buster.

Dwayne closes his eyes and squints.

"You ain't goin' to the toilet right here, are ya?" asks Buster, looking rather put off.

"No, I'm usin' *The Shhh* to visualize the money."

Buster rolls his eyes.

"Get real, Dwayne. You're an embarrassment to the Wide name. When's a problem like this ever stopped the Wide boys?"

"There was the race horse deal in Brighton," recalls Dwayne with a grimace.

"True."

"Then the truckload of rubber sink plugs in Luton. And the three thousand towels that we thought were beach towels and turned out to be sanitary towels…"

"Yeah, alright, alright." Buster sighs and looks at Dwayne's strained expression. "It's alright. You don't have to think of any more."

"I'm not. I really need the bathroom!" Dwayne pulls the swimming goggles from his pocket and puts them on. Buster walks over to his car. "Where are you goin'?"

"To see a man about a dog."

With buttocks clenched tighter than a Scotsman's hand on a two-pence piece, Dwayne cycles Aurora's pink bicycle along the shoulder of the busy road in the direction of home. His stomach gurgles and he feels the need to use the bathroom even more urgently than before. Just to add insult to colon injury, a headwind makes the journey that much more challenging.

On the same road, traveling in the opposite direction to Dwayne, is a beat-up 1976 VW van. Its brown exterior is mostly due to rust. The van splutters and coughs its way up the highway at an exhausting forty-seven miles-per-hour.

Inside the van, a jubilant Carl drives, while Greg sits in the passenger seat clutching a tatty duffle bag to his padded bra. The two of them are wearing the dresses and wigs that they picked out the previous night.

"We did it, we actually did it!" exclaims Greg, looking down at the duffle bag, his tall frame almost bent in half to fit in the van.

"Went like clockwork," agrees Carl, pulling off his wig and scratching his bald head.

He keeps glancing in the rearview mirror, but he cannot see anything out of the back window due to the dark tinting that is scratched and bubbled in many places. The side mirror on his door is no better; its shattered face is kept together with clear tape, resulting in multiple small views all at different angles.

Greg delves into the duffle bag and pulls out several wads of money. They look to each other and excitedly scream like teenage girls seeing their pop idol.

At the same exact moment, Dwayne is visualizing being home and sitting on the toilet, but it is of no use. Aurora's high-fiber diet and cycling make for a deadly combination. Nature is not only calling, but it's screaming, "NOW!" He pulls the bike off the busy road and over into a grassy verge sprinkled with shrubs and lays it down. As cars stream past, Dwayne desperately looks around before darting off into the scrub frantically tugging at the belt around his shorts.

Back in the VW van, Carl laughs uproariously while Greg pulls his wig off, his unkempt hair springing up, like a Jack-in-the-box. They are both still wearing makeup and look like they are returning from a cross-dressing convention.

"Right, let's get home and get this stuff off, then celebrate with a brewski as we count the money," suggests Carl.

"You were amazing," says Greg, his voice full of admiration.

"No, no." Carl is almost blushing. "Really? Was I?"

"Yeah, you were great."

"Didn't think I overdid it on the makeup?"

"No, no," replies Greg. "You looked like a real señorita with those thick eyebrows."

"Well, you, you were just terrific as a woman, too," says Carl, feeling like he should return the compliment.

"You think? Not too tall?"

"Weeeell…"

From behind comes the sound of a fast-approaching siren. The men look at one another other and then back through the rear window of the van. The bubbled and scratched dark window tinting reveals only the distorted flashing of blue, red and yellow lights.

"Cops!" cries Greg, panicking.

"Stay calm," instructs Carl.

"We've been busted. I can't go to jail."

"Shut up!" Carl looks in the broken side mirror. All he can see are multiple versions of different-colored flashing lights approaching at speed.

"Whatta we gonna do?" Greg looks around frantically, still clutching the duffle bag of money. "You said it was gonna be alright, everything would be fine."

The sirens and flashing lights are almost on their tail.

By now, Dwayne is squatting in the shrubs, feeling much better. He looks up into the sky basking in the sunshine of a lovely day and seems quite content as he relieves himself. He hears the traffic speed by and does not take much heed of the approaching siren. He looks around for something to use as toilet paper. He sees a mass of grass and plants and grabs a handful.

"Now what?" Greg cries out, his eyes wide. "Do you know what they do to tall people in prison?" Carl is also panicking, but quietly. "Faster, go faster!" commands Greg.

"It's doing forty-seven already!" Carl's foot is flat to the floor. He looks in the shattered wing mirror, but the vibrations of the van at top speed make it almost impossible for him to discern how many police cars are following them.

Greg winds down his window and emits a grunt.

Carl looks over just in time to see Greg lean out of the window and with his long arms throw the duffle bag of money high in the air, over the van, clearing the cars on the other side of the road.

"Noooooooooooo!" Carl watches as the duffle bag sails through the air towards the shrubs.

Dwayne, having finished using the grass and local plant as toilet paper, stands to pull up his trousers. Out of nowhere, a duffle bag hits him square in the chest, pushing him backwards and almost knocking him over. The duffle bag falls to the ground near his feet.

In the van, a horrified Carl is looking at Greg with disbelief.

"What the hell did you just do?"

Carl glances out of his window as an ambulance speeds past them. The medic in the passenger seat flips him the bird.

"Thank God. It's an ambulance and not a cop car," says Greg.

"Thank God?" Carl is incredulous. "You just threw the money out of the window!"

"If they find it on us, they'll know we did it."

"Oh, like the women's clothes aren't a giveaway?" Carl slams on the brakes and pulls the van over to the side of the road, as other cars drive past. "We have to go back and get it." He kills the engine.

Carl leaps out of the van looking like a transsexual on chemotherapy. He looks back to where Greg threw the duffle bag.

In the shrubs, a confused Dwayne fastens the belt on his shorts as he stares at the duffle bag near his feet. Curious, he picks it up and opens it. When he sees that it is full of wads of cash, a large smile appears on his face.

"It works! *The Shhh* really works! Thank you!" He looks to the skies and holds up the duffle bag in joy.

Carl sees the distant figure of a man hoisting the duffle bag and then clutching it to his chest. Squinting to get a sharper look, he notices the figure pick up what appears to be a lady's pink bicycle, straddle it and cycle back onto the shoulder of the road.

"Oh, no."

Carl doubles back to the van, gets in, slams it into drive and speeds away, as best a 1976 VW van can.

"Some guy has the bag!" he shouts at Greg, as he drives. "Just gotta find a place to turn round." He looks at Greg with disdain. "You just threw half a million dollars out the window. Half a million dollars!"

"How did I know it was an ambulance? If you had a better van, then…"

"The whole point of stealing the money was so I could buy a better van. How can I buy a better van if the person who helped me steal the money throws it out of the window?" Carl shakes his head. "I knew I should have done this on my own."

Palm-tree-lined Rodeo Drive in Beverly Hills is the epicenter of haute couture, expensive designer clothes and accessories that only the genuinely rich and pretentiously faux rich can afford. The remainder just window shop, many unable to afford the window, let alone anything behind it. Plastic cards match plastic faces, pulled tight by the best surgeons in Hollywood in a vain attempt to look like some startled movie star.

Skinny women walk skinnier dogs clad in designer doggie-wear that costs more than an average person might spend on their own clothes. The street is lined with Gucci, Ralph Lauren, Cartier, Harry Winston and Lacoste amongst many other fine shops. The world may be going to the dogs, but these dogs are going to Rodeo Drive.

In amongst the shops is a sprinkling of small art galleries. In one of these, Buster places a piece of colorful abstract art on an easel inside the gallery's plush back office. It appears to be a framed painting of a dog, but only if you squint.

On the other side of the ornate desk sits a man in his fifties. He is well-dressed, portly, with short hair dyed far too black for his age. Buster notices that the gallery manager is wearing a lot of jewelry, including a pair of diamond earrings, and wonders if he bats for the other team.

"Ten thousand, you say?" asks the manager. He takes off his glasses and places one earpiece in his mouth, in deep thought.

"Euros, or whatever that is in dollars." Buster is trying to sound more educated than he is.

"And what's the painter's name?"

"Renée Coulthard."

"French?"

"Could be, if you like," replies Buster.

"And how did you come by this exquisite piece of art?"

In his mind, Buster can picture young Rachel sitting at the table in their cluttered living room, using her fingers to paint over a cheap print of a Constable that he picked up for free on Craigslist.

"Er, friend of the family back in England, to be honest, Guv."

"And you are who again?"

"Bust..., er, Barry Wide from *Wide World of Art*." He hands the manager a flimsy card that Rachel designed and printed using her computer. He looks at the card, then stands and walks over to the painting. He puts on his glasses to take a closer look.

"The frame's a bit understated," he remarks.

Buster had spotted the frame months ago in a pile of trash behind a thrift shop in Van Nuys. He had punched out the paint-by-numbers atrocity to make room for Rachel's masterpiece.

"That's so as not to distract from the paintin' itself," explains Buster, thinking on his feet.

"This painting has such unique qualities. It's as if the artist has abandoned, or at least ignored, all technical and conventional methods of painting to produce a work with almost Neanderthal naiveté."

"My words exactly," says Buster.

"Is she prolific?"

Buster looks confused for a moment.

"Er, no. No, she's got all her arms and legs."

"I mean, does she paint a lot?"

"Oh, no. She prefers quality over quantity. Hence, the rarity and high market value."

"Shame."

"Well, no, not really." Buster starts backpedaling. "I do have several pieces of hers like this that have yet to be put on the market."

"And you say you have a letter of authenticity? That's unusual for an unknown artist."

"It is? Oh, yes, it is. We anticipate big things from her in the future so we want to be protected from the very beginnin'."

"Very wise and forward-thinking of you."

Buster pulls an envelope from his pocket and hands it to the manager, who opens it and scans the page. The letter of authenticity looks genuine and even has a round embossed stamp on it. Rachel designed the page in Photoshop then printed it. Buster himself had pressed the corner of the paper down hard on a Texan Steer belt buckle to make the embossed mark.

The manager looks up and smiles at Buster.

"The decision will not be up to me, of course. I will need to show it to the gallery owner, who isn't here today. Can I keep the painting and show him when he returns?"

"Er, better not. I'll come back. I do have other interested parties."

"I see. Let me make a quick call then." The manager walks back to his desk.

An excited and fully relieved Dwayne, pedals fast on his bike along the road. He is wearing his swimming goggles and has his arms through the handles of the duffle bag that sits on his back like Quasimodo's hump. Having taken his relief break, cycling is much easier. Cars zoom by as he approaches the more densely populated part of Calabasas.

Having turned the dilapidated van around, Carl now drives as fast as it will go. Using the fast lane is merely wishful thinking on his part. Impatient drivers keep passing them.

"So, what are we looking for?" asks Greg.

Carl looks at him, dumbfounded.

"A guy on a bike with our duffle bag, moron."

Carl continues to scan ahead as Greg looks to his right. A passing car reveals a glimpse of Dwayne on his pink bike. Greg keeps his eyes on him, as Dwayne peels off the main road onto a side street and into town.

"Did he have dark hair, swimming goggles and a girl's bike?" asks Greg innocently. "If so, he just turned off."

Carl slams on the brakes. Car horns honk in protest. Carl and Greg lurch forward as the van comes to a grinding halt. He slams it in reverse and drives illegally backwards down the road to the turn-off.

A breathless Dwayne cycles off the main road and into an up-market shopping center built around a parking lot. People look at Dwayne strangely as he rides by in search of a payphone. Spotting one, he leaps off the pink bike, letting it fall to the ground nearby. He fumbles in his pocket for coins. Retrieving his one and only quarter, he deposits it in the slot and dials.

Buster stands near the painting, looking around the ostentatious office, as the manager talks on the phone.

"Yes, yes. I see. Well, I've certainly not seen anything quite like this in a while now. It's didactic, yet visually vernacular. The palette creates a temperate soliloquy of strokes with the innocence of an infantile progression."

Buster is trying to understand if this is a good or bad thing when his cell phone rings to the theme tune to the film "The Sting". He quickly takes the call as the manager continues with his own call.

"Hello, Wide World of Art," Buster says in greeting.

Dwayne, too excited to remove his goggles, stands at the payphone, duffle bag on his back.

"Buster. It's me. We hit the jackpot. I got the money. I got the money!" shouts Dwayne excitedly and not thinking that someone might be within earshot.

Buster is half-listening to the curator and half-listening to Dwayne.

"I see, sir, and how much as we talkin' about here?" he asks, not showing even a twitch of excitement.

"A shed load. Well, a duffle bag load," replies Dwayne. "More than I can count in a month of Sundays. It's like manna from heaven. In fact, that's where it came from. *The Shhh* works, my brother, it really works!"

"I see. And where are you now, sir?" asks Buster.

"The posh mini-mall in Calabasas, near the cinema." Something catches his eye. He looks round as a teenager dressed in a loose T-shirt and baggy shorts quickly picks up the pink bicycle from the ground, straddles it and frantically rides away. "Hey you!" shouts Dwayne. "Get off my bike!" Dwayne takes off after the youth, but one arm is still holding the payphone, so he can only move a few feet. "Oy!" He brings the receiver back to his ear. "Some bastard's gone and stole my bike!"

Buster holds the mobile phone away from his ear as Dwayne is now shouting "Stop, thief!" at the top of his lungs.

The gallery manager finishes his call and looks up. Buster realizes the man can hear Dwayne shouting through the phone.

"A very excited client," Buster says with a smile. He brings the cell phone back to his ear. "Would you like me to bring the paintin' to you, sir?" Buster removes the phone from his ear as Dwayne continues shouting, then replaces it. "Very good, sir. I'll be there shortly." Buster hangs up. He smiles at the curator and slides his painting under one arm. "Call me."

Carl drives the VW van along the streets of Calabasas, as he and Greg scan intently around them for the thief.

At the entrance to the mini-mall, the youth shoots out into traffic on the stolen pink bicycle. He looks a little like Dwayne, with dark hair and shorts.

"There!" points Greg, slamming his finger into the windscreen.

"Got him," replies Carl, tight-lipped and ready to seek revenge. "I'll pull up ahead then we'll jump him."

"Right."

Carl speeds ahead, overtaking the youth on the bike. Fifty feet ahead, Carl screeches the van to the curb. Both he and Greg leap out.

The bike thief speeds towards them, momentarily confused by the sight of two enraged men wearing makeup and dresses. He is even more confused when Carl and Greg leap on him and force him onto the ground. He comes crashing down onto the grassy patch of the sidewalk, the bicycle still between his legs. Carl and Greg regain their footing then hold the youth down.

"Give it back!" shouts Carl.

"Take it. Take it! I didn't mean to steal it," whimpers the petrified youth.

Carl and Greg pat him down all over, searching for the duffle bag but it is not there.

"Where is it?"

The youth looks confused and a little concerned.

"Er, between my legs!"

In the bedroom of Tiffany's cluttered apartment, Buster, having removed his jacket and loosened his tie, stands with Dwayne, looking down at the bed. On it is the duffle bag and, next to it, wads of money bound in paper ties denoting $10,000 bundles. Only one tie is broken and the money lies loose on the bedcover.

"And you're tellin' me it just fell out of the sky?" asks Buster, unconvinced.

"Like from nowhere. Right on top of me," says Dwayne. "I tell you, it's all because of *The Shhh*. If you try it, maybe we'll get even more."

"Well, it must have come from somewhere. A bag of money doesn't just fall out of the sky."

"It does if you believe in abundance," says Dwayne self-righteously. "Wherever it came from, it's ours now. Finders, keepers and all that."

"How much did you say is there?"

"Four hundred and ninety nine thousand nine hundred and ninety nine dollars and seventy five cents." He looks at Buster and shrugs. "I bought a pack of gum waitin' for you."

Buster retrieves a quarter from his pocket and tosses it on to the pile.

"Half a mil!" he says with a big smile. They look to each other and laugh out loud.

"You wait 'til I tell Aurora that *The Shhh* works and that I found …"

"No, no, no! You can't tell anyone about this," insists Buster. "Not right now, anyway."

"Why not?"

"First of all, they won't believe us. Secondly, I wouldn't put it past your Aurora to want a commission and turn it into some multi-level marketin' scheme. No. We need to keep quiet about this for a while. Let me do some thinkin'."

Dwayne scratches his backside and looks uncomfortable.

"What's up with you?" Buster asks.

"Dunno. But my bum is itchin' like crazy. Can you drive me home?"

Incense smoke tumbles and somersaults into the air, disturbing the parrot that is perched on a branch of a rubber tree. Although it is daytime, the bamboo blinds are drawn closed. Scented candles give Aurora's living room a mystical and surreal ambiance.

Aurora sits opposite her client, each in the Lotus position, on a brightly colored, tie-dye rug upon the bare wooden floor. They are surrounded by recycled cloth beanbags, Buddha effigies, spiritual symbols, and a bunny with a twitching nose.

Aurora is wearing a gossamer caftan, while the older woman wears a modern tracksuit. They sit with hands resting on knees, palms facing upwards, finger and thumb touching in the universal sign for spiritualism. Between them are Tarot cards, a pad of paper and a pen. Soft mystical music plays in the background, accompanied by the sound of running water from the miniature waterfall in the kitchen.

"Power comes from our inner strength. Only too often, women lose their power to men and don't feel as though they can reach their full potential."

"Full potential, yes," agrees the woman, her eyes closed.

"Go deep into your inner self and find the woman you were before you met your man."

"Going deep, right," echoes the woman.

"Then, when you've found that inner self – reconnect."

"Reconnecting. Got it."

Aurora can feel her cell phone vibrating under her caftan. She opens one eye and looks down at the screen. The woman opens her eyes.

"Eyes closed, connect with the one," insists Aurora.

"The one what?"

"The one that is you." Aurora's voice is slow and patronizing. She checks her text message and types an answer as she talks. "Now, with eyes shut tight, imagine the power that you've regained, the person you once were. Remember that you are nobody unless you have your power. Someone with no power is a nobody."

The door opens and in walks Dwayne the best he can with an itchy bottom. Aurora's client opens her eyes and looks at Dwayne.

"Who's that?" she asks.

"Nobody," says Aurora.

In the dilapidated bungalow in West Hills, Carl stares out the window onto the dark street below. He sighs then scratches his shaved head in thought. On the sofa, looking carefree, Greg eats popcorn while watching a zombie movie on television. He has an

affinity for monster movies, perhaps because his father had a
striking resemblance to Herman Munster.

Carl sullenly walks away from the window.

"I guess that didn't go too well," says Greg glancing over with
a mouthful of popcorn.

"Actually it went really, really well until you threw half a
million dollars out of the window!" snaps Carl.

"We didn't get arrested though, did we?"

"Ambulances don't arrest people."

"What are we going to do?"

"I've no idea." Carl walks over and snatches the television
remote from Greg and changes the channel. "And stop watching
that." The channel changes to another station where the news is
being broadcast by a smartly-dressed, all-American-looking
anchorman.

"…to a record high over Vegas. In local news, a Ron's
supermarket in Calabasas was held up earlier today. Thieves
walked away with half a million dollars in cash from the safe.
Police have little to go on except an eyewitness account by the
manager. Mandy Ashton has this report."

The image on the television changes to an attractive reporter
inside the supermarket manager's office. It is difficult to see much,
as almost half of the screen is obscured by the broadcaster's logo,
the time clock, the reporter's name on a wide banner, the current
temperature, and a scrolling text indicating which story is up next.

"Scott Linus, the manager of this Ron's Supermarket in
Calabasas, was held at gunpoint this morning when two women
walked into his office and forced him to open the safe and hand
over half a million dollars in cash," says the reporter in an earnest
voice. "I have Mr. Linus here with me now." She turns to him.
"Can you tell us what happened?"

"Two women came into my office under the pretense of a
complaint, pulled guns on me and forced me to open the safe that
contained this week's takings."

In the cramped bedroom of Tiffany's apartment, Buster sits
motionless on the edge of the bed, watching the same news on a
small TV perched on the cluttered dresser. He is helping Tiffany
with the inventory of all the free goods crammed into the other
rooms, while Rachel is playing scrabble with a scruffy homeless

man on the floor.

"They didn't look dangerous, being women," the manager is telling the reporter on the TV. "Until they pulled guns and threatened me with them. I was in fear of my life."

Buster stares at the screen putting two and two together. Rachel totals up the score from the homeless man's word.

"Hagiography. Well done. That's a fifty-six point word," says Rachel, as she writes down the score. The homeless man looks pleased with himself.

"How did you feel?" asks the TV reporter.

"I was petrified. I really thought they were going to kill me if I didn't do what they demanded," says Scott, hamming it up for the cameras, as if his thespian efforts might gain him a Screen Actors Guild card.

"What shall I sell these breast pumps for?" asks Tiffany.

"Shhhhh!" implores Buster, glued to the television.

"I also talked to the supervisor who spoke with the two women just before the robbery," says the reporter to camera. "I asked her to describe the two robbers."

The screen switches to a shot of the customer service supervisor, Lawanda.

"Well, they were both white and, without being too unkind, these women were *ugly*. And they had no sense of style."

"Well, that's not nice, is it?" says Greg, taking umbrage at the criticism being hurled at him from the TV screen. "Not like you're a raving beauty, dear."

"Their shoes didn't match their dresses and their earrings were nasty clip-ons," continues Lawanda.

"I told you we should have gotten our ears pierced! But no, nar, nar, nar, nar, nar!" mocks Greg, shoveling popcorn into his mouth.

Back in Tiffany's bedroom, Buster is glued to the news program as the penny, or rather, the half a million dollars, drops. He stands up, grabs his keys and wallet, then walks to the door.

"Where are you going at this hour?" asks Tiffany.

"I gotta see Dwayne about somethin'."

"Could you bring back a take-away for dinner? I can't get to the kitchen for all the boxes of unwanted Richard Simmons videos of 'Wriggling with the Wrinklies'. "

"Yeah, okay." Buster straddles the clutter in the bedroom and leaves, while Rachel places her tiles down on the Scrabble board.

"Diatribe: to rant or argue. Twenty four points for me," she says. "Your turn."

In their living room, Carl and Greg watch the rest of the news story.

"So there you have it. Two women held up a supermarket today and left with half a million dollars in cash. Back to you at the studio."

"Thank you, Mandy, for that report," says the anchorman. "In other news today, government archives confirmed that George W. Bush was reported to be the first President ever to officially be found illiterate in seven different languages..."

Hearing a loud knock at the door, Carl and Greg look to each other. There is another knock, this one even louder. Carl turns off the TV and gingerly creeps up to the door. He opens it to reveal Scott Linus, the manager of Ron's Supermarket, standing in the doorway with a stoic look on his face.

"You gonna let me in or what?" asks Scott in his Texan drawl and with a beaming smile. As soon as Carl opens the door a crack, Scott pushes past him and strides into the living room. "Bought it hook, line and sinker, eh, boys?" Scott says. "Ha! Did you see me on the news?" He playfully punches Carl then Greg in the stomach like some college jock. "That's an Oscar-winning performance, if ever I saw one." He claps his hands. "Not even the cops suspect anything, since I called the security systems people yesterday to say that all the cameras were down." He taps his forehead with his finger. "Always thinking, thinking, thinking, I am." He looks around. "So where is it?"

"What?" says Greg, stalling.

"The lost city of Atlantis," replies Scott. "The money of course. Where's the money? Under the mattress, in the sofa?"

"Er, we don't have it."

"You mean it's in a safe place somewhere?"

"I mean, we don't have it. Greg threw it out the window."

Scott takes a second to comprehend.

"Out of what window?"

"The van window," says Greg. "We were being chased. So I threw it out the window so we wouldn't get caught with it."

"Chased?"

"The police were..." starts Carl.

"No, no, it was an ambulance, remember?" says Greg. "We thought it was a police car, but it wasn't....it was....a....er..,"

Carl gives Greg a dirty look to shut him up.

Scott looks from one to the other.

"Well, where is it now?" His smile has vanished.

"We think some guy picked it up."

"Some guy? What guy? I mean, what guy?" Scott is getting annoyed.

"We don't know. Some guy on a pink bike wearing swimming goggles. We chased him, but when we found him, it was someone else on a pink bike," says Carl.

"Amazing how many guys ride pink bikes in Calabasas," says Greg innocently.

Scott shakes his head, failing to contain his anger.

"Are you trying to tell me, that this cleverly thought out plan of mine, that took months to prepare, is all for nothing because you pea brains then threw the money out of the van window?"

Carl quietly points to Greg, deflecting the blame.

Scott puts his hands on his head and paces the room dumbfounded.

"I don't believe it. I don't freakin' believe it." He stops pacing. "Where's this man now?"

"That's the funny thing, we don't know." Greg shrugs his shoulders.

"But I got a pretty good look at him," says Carl. "When he picked up the duffle bag, I got to see him."

"Oh, well, if you got a pretty good look at him, it should be easy enough to spot him in amongst the gazillion people that are wandering around LA," rants Scott.

"You'd think," says Greg.

Scott looks down at the floor and shakes his head, thinking. Then he turns a menacing gaze at the two of them.

"Hang on, hang on. Why am I believing anything you two say? How do I know that you haven't stashed the cash somewhere and are just lying to me?" Scott gets in Carl's face. "Just because we were roommates once, doesn't mean that I won't do you some harm if I find out that you're trying to double-cross me and keep my part of the money."

"We don't have it, honest. We don't know where it is."

"Actually, I don't care if you do or don't know where it is." Scott turns sharply to look at Greg and finds himself facing Greg's chest. He looks up. "You owe me two hundred and fifty grand. I don't care where you get it from." He walks to the door. "And, I better get it real soon or there'll be trouble." He slams the door shut as he leaves.

Aurora is home alone, contorted like a pretzel in a yoga pose on the living room floor. Thunder and lightning sounds emanate from the iPod system. The bamboo curtains are still closed and candles burn to illuminate the room. There is a knock at the door.

"Come in," she calls out.

Buster opens the door and walks in to a familiar sight.

"Oh, it's you," says Aurora, disappointed. "Mind the tortoise, he's got an upset stomach, so there might be turtle barf on the floor."

"Where's Dwayne?"

"He's not feeling too good, either. His aura is displaced. He's having some Dwayne time in the bedroom."

Buster walks through the living room to the bedroom. He opens the door and flicks on the light, revealing the bedroom's Middle Eastern-themed décor: plants, spiritual paintings, dark cloths draped from the ceiling and walls, and a large bed piled high with Arabic styled pillows. Dwayne lies facedown on the bed, trousers and underpants round his ankles with a hand towel covering his backside.

"What the hell happened to you?" asks Buster.

"Poison oak I think," mutters Dwayne, scratching his backside. "Must have been in the grass I used to…"

"Yeah, yeah, alright, I get it," says Buster.

Dwayne tries to move, but all he can do is glance over to his brother.

"What have you done with the money?"

"Shhhhhh!"

"I know. It's all because of *The Shhh*," says Dwayne.

"No. I mean, keep ya voice down!" Buster looks around as if someone else were in the room with them.

"Where's the money now?"

35

"It's safe under my bed where nobody can find it." Buster crouches down to Dwayne's level. "I just wanna make sure that you're keepin' your mouth shut about the money. I don't think Aurora would understand exactly that it was blind luck or somethin'."

"It's amazin' how this positive thinkin' works, Buster. You really gotta try it. I just thought about wantin' more money and *bam*, there it was."

"Yeah, amazin'," replies Buster, not wanting to burst Dwayne's bubble. He cares for his simple brother, but is aware of Aurora's influence on him. "You still don't have a TV, right?"

"You know I don't. Why, you got an extra one I can have?" Dwayne seems excited. "I miss BBC America and the reruns of 'Are You Being Served.'"

Buster ignores his request.

"So here's the story we're gonna use about the money. As far as anyone's concerned, we have an investor, a guy from Texas. Got it? That way, the girls'll never have to meet him. A silent partner, that kind of thing."

"Okay. A Texan investor that can't speak. Got it."

Buster seems concerned.

"If anyone asks, just let me explain, alright?"

"Ooh!" Dwayne winces and points to the tube on the table. "Ointment!" Buster hands him the tube but Dwayne demurs. "You couldn't just...you know? I can't reach."

Disgusted, Buster stands and walks to the door.

"Get Aurora to use those healin' hands of hers."

# CHAPTER 3

It is another scorching California morning, as the sun pokes its nose over the layer of smog. You know you are in Los Angeles when you wake up in the morning and hear the birds coughing. The traffic is gridlocked on the 101 Freeway and talk radio spreads gossip about celebrities' indiscretions, some of which have yet to happen. Hollywood is all about image. Some local councils are so aware of their image they have been known to Botox the brow of a hill.

Michael, the real estate agent, stands by his shiny car beside the vacant lot of land that might be the location for Buster and Dwayne's pub. He looks at his watch and adjusts his sunglasses. It is not yet ten o'clock, but the temperature is already close to ninety degrees.

Buster drives up in Tiffany's old Ford and parks next to Michael's car. The brothers get out, Dwayne more gingerly than Buster, who is clutching the duffle bag. They stroll over to Michael. Dwayne is walking very strangely, bow legged and with his hips thrust forward, as though he is riding a horse.

"Mornin'," says Buster. He is dressed casually in shorts and a tank top.

"Another fine day in paradise." Michael notices that Dwayne is walking with a waddle. "What's up with John Wayne, here?"

"Er, new underwear," explains Dwayne, off the cuff.

"I got your call. You were quick finding the money."

"Turned out to be easier to get than we thought." Buster glances at Dwayne then surveys the plot of land. "So, this is it?"

"Yup. All one and a half acres of prime real estate, permit-ready, stamped and approved for commercial and residential construction. You want to walk the lot?"

"Nah. We got our architect plans. We'll make it fit."

"So, let's do this, then. I've got the paperwork here for you."
Michael reaches in through his open car window and pulls out a
file. "Sign where those strange plastic pointer things are." He
hands the file to Buster. "Check or cashier's check will do. When
the check clears, then you get the deeds."

"You take cash?" asks Buster.

"Cash? As in cash money, cash?"

"As in cash, don't tell the taxman cash, yes," replies Buster.

"Yes, but it's still a hundred and fifty big ones, plus my cut of
twenty-five on top."

"Twenty for cash."

Michael considers this.

"Done."

Buster screws up his face.

"How do I know you're not makin' a cut off of the farmer, as
well?"

"You don't," says Michael in all seriousness. "Look, you know
the land's worth a hell of a lot more. You're paying me to get it
cheap for you. Plus, some of that commission is going to my
brother-in-law down at the permit office, for expediting your
building permit and liquor license, if you know what I mean."

Buster looks around then hands over the duffel bag of money.

"It's all in there."

"Where d'you get the money from so quickly?" asks Michael,
as he takes the duffel bag and puts it in his car.

"Shrewd business dealin', my friend." Buster smiles.

"Well, sign away and we can get this wrapped up." Michael
looks around cautiously, as if this were a drug deal.

Buster places the paperwork on the car hood and starts signing.

Dwayne looks at Michael with some curiosity and misplaced
envy.

"So, what do you think of the new Batman film? You know,
with that new actor guy. Not like the good old days, eh?"

Michael looks at Dwayne, not sure whether he should burst his
bubble or not.

"He came to me for advice. Taught him everything I knew
about the character. Stuff you can't find in comic books or on the
pages of a script," Michael says, going with the flow.

"So why are you doin' this kind of work?"

"I'm between lawyers right now. Hollywood's a bitch, you know. An ungrateful bitch at that. Loves you when you're up, ignores you when you're down. Had a good run though. Better than most in this town."

Buster hands over the signed papers.

"There you go. Now what about the buildin' contractor you talked of?"

"Waiting for your call." Michael hands him a business card.

Buster takes it and looks at it.

"Good, is he?"

"Cheap, very cheap. Not only that, but as an incentive, with the market slumping the way it is, he's willing to pay the first six months of your mortgage just to get the business."

"Really?" says Buster, impressed. "That could be useful. So, when can we start buildin'?"

"Sort that out with him. Permits and licenses are all done, so you can start building tomorrow, as far as I'm concerned."

Buster looks to Dwayne and they share a smile.

On the way to see the contractor, Dwayne fidgets in the passenger seat, due to his itching condition.

"You alright?" asks his brother..

"Yeah, gettin' better, I think." He looks to Buster. "So, a hundred and seventy down out of five hundred grand leaves..?" Dwayne tries to do the math in his head, but gives up. "Not that much to build a pub and furnish it."

"Enough to get a contractor and more than enough to get a mortgage for the rest."

"See, *The Shhh* works, Buster. It works."

"All I see is my brother being conned by a grifter and gettin' an itchy arse for doin' it."

"What about the five hundred G's? That came from visualizin' abundance. I knew we needed it, I visualized it and it arrived. You can't deny that!"

"Your bird, Janet…"

"Aurora."

"Whatever. Well, how come she ain't visualized abundance and made it work for her, if she's so hot on this *Shhh* thing, then?"

"She has. Look at her apartment."

"Exactly. For someone who makes eighty bucks an hour, I don't see where it goes. Candles and plant food don't cost much. She don't turn the lights on, no TV, no car, no computer and she eats rabbit food that can't cost much. Either she ain't doin' as well as she says, or she's got a nest egg of dosh hidden away somewhere."

"She's got a good heart."

"She's got you wrapped round her finger is what she's got," Buster says, keeping his hands on the wheel.

"No, she don't." Dwayne thinks for a moment. "Well, it is her apartment, and I don't cook, so I guess we do what she wants back there. But outside her gaff, I'm my own boss."

"Oh, yeah? Prove it."

"Okay. Next McDonald's, I'm buyin'."

Buster pulls into the parking lot of an industrial area of warehouses and small offices. The brothers get out, crush the McDonald's packets and toss them into the back seat. Buster tucks the roll of architect plans under one arm and leads the way in his usual cocky swagger. Dwayne, clutching a plastic bag of money, walks like he has a baseball bat inserted where the California sun does not shine.

The man they have come to see is Olaf Ashanov, a portly man in his late fifties of dubious heritage and breeding. He is sitting in a small office, behind his cluttered Ikea desk, with the Venetian blinds down on the windows. On his desk, flanked by two bottles of Stolichnaya vodka and glasses, sits a gorgeous blonde secretary wearing a short skirt and low-cut blouse. She is not very bright, but that is not what Olaf hired her for. It is unlikely that she could create a spark if she were to rub her two brain cells together, but quite possibly if she tried with her breasts. Not that Olaf is a beacon of intellectual prowess. If an alien were to abduct him and conduct tests, they would probably conclude that evolution was in a regressive stage.

Olaf sports a bright, multi-colored, Hawaiian short-sleeve shirt, a deep, Mediterranean tan and large-framed sunglasses. His most prominent feature is a rather obvious and cheap black hairpiece that clashes with his graying sideburns.

The secretary sits cross-legged, filing the nails on Olaf's left hand, as he talks to someone through the Bluetooth pressed to his ear. His other hand is firmly grasping a glass of vodka.

"She working out real fine," says Olaf in what sounds like a Russian accent. "She busy doing some filing for me right now." He looks up and smiles at her. She smiles back and files another nail. "Look Vladimir, that Polish guy in Van Nuys keeps calling me about some four-by-two. I don't know what he talks about. Is he building an ark? I thought the animals went in two by two?" He listens as the person on the other end explains. Olaf takes a sip of his drink. "Why didn't he say wood then? Just take it from the other house. When the dry wall is up, who is going to notice if a few uprights are missing?" He takes another sip. "If I was supposed to understand it, then it wouldn't be called building *code* would it?" There is a knock at the door. "I have to go. We talk later." He taps his Bluetooth to end the call and indicates to his secretary to answer the door.

She dutifully slips off the desk, adjusts her short skirt and opens the doors to reveal Buster and Dwayne.

"Hi. Buster and Dwayne Wide to see a Mr...," Buster peers at the card. "Ashan-an-onin-ov-ov, or somethin' like that."

"Ashanov!" calls out Olaf.

"Bless you," says Dwayne.

"Come, come." Olaf beckons them closer with his manicured hand, hiding the glass of vodka behind some binders. The secretary opens the door wider and they step inside. "You be friends of Michael, right?"

"Right."

"You sound English."

"We are," replies Buster proudly. "You Russian?"

"I can be, if you want." He smiles at them both. "You want coffee?"

"No thanks," replies Buster."

"Good. June, go get men coffee."

"It's April," she corrects.

"Who cares what month it is. Go get men coffee." He looks to them. "Black, white, sugar?"

"Nothin' thanks," says Dwayne.

"Good. Black no sugar," says Olaf. When April leaves, closing the door behind her, he adds, "Please, sit, sit."

"I'll stand if that's okay." Dwayne is still feeling tender. Buster sits in front of the desk holding the architectural plans on his lap.

Olaf leans forward and removes his sunglasses, revealing two white, untanned patches of skin around his eyes.

"Now, Michael tells me you want pub built, is that right?"

"Yeah. You had much experience with pubs?"

Olaf glances at the bottle of vodka on the desk.

"Some," he says, then smiles, displaying rows of overly-white teeth. "What you got for me?"

Buster stands and unfurls the surveyor's and architect's plans on the desk. He uses a vodka bottle to keep them from rolling back up.

"This is the plot of land and this is the pub we want to build."

Olaf examines the plans in detail, running his finger up and down the lines of the architect's drawings.

"Uh huh! I see. Got it. Right. Uh, huh. Interesting."

"Make any sense to you?" asks Dwayne.

"No. No idea what all these blue squiggly lines for, but I got guy that does." Olaf leans back in his chair.

"What do you do as a contractor then?" asks Buster, confused.

"I am like conductor of orchestra. I don't know how to play instruments, but I pull in all experienced people who do and make it work for the client at a very reasonable rate."

"You any good?"

"I'm cheapest, fastest contractor in area. Ask anyone. And I am man who stands by his convictions – except for that one fraud case in Woodland Hills. That I didn't do."

"Our friend Michael says that you also pay the first six months of a mortgage," says Dwayne, looking down on Olaf and his nylon wig.

"That's usually for houses that have been built on spec, rather than contracted. It is incentive to bring in first-time buyers." When he smiles, his facial skin crumples and creases like used greaseproof paper. "But in your case I can make exception, seeing as how you friends of Michael."

"How much do you think it will cost to build this and how long?" asks Buster.

"Put it this way. How much you got and when do you want it by?"

"Quarter of a mil, cash. Soon as possible. The land is ours as of an hour ago."

"Let's say all construction costs are half a mil. You can get the rest as mortgage?" asks Olaf.

"No problem. I can give you a hundred G's right now to get the ball rollin'."

Dwayne drops the plastic bag filled with wads of money onto the desk.

Olaf's eyes widen and his smile broadens.

"Then I'll be first drinking customer in about two months from now." Olaf looks serious for a moment. "To keep cheap, no receipts, right?"

Buster smiles at Olaf.

"I understand your way of thinkin'. But I do want a contract with all that we just talked about on it. For the bank, you understand."

A few minutes later, Buster and Dwayne are walking to the car. Buster is shaking the ink dry on the contract in his hand. Dwayne carries the plans and surveyor maps.

"So, when we pay him out for construction, that'll leave us eighty grand to paint, decorate and stock the bar with booze," Buster says.

"He looked a little dodgy, I thought," says Dwayne, softly.

"Of course he is, that's why I like him. Keep ya friends close and ya dodgy contractor even closer."

"Think he'll rip us off?"

"I don't doubt it. But I got a cunnin' plan to even the score if he does."

"What's that?"

"It involves the biggest crooks and loan sharks known to man. We're goin' to the bank!"

The sound of a bullfrog's occasional croaking pierces the tranquil sounds of rain from the iPod player.

Buster and Dwayne sit with Rachel, Tiffany and Aurora in their usual places at the wooden table in the middle of Aurora's equatorial living room, eating dinner. They are joined by a homeless man, probably only thirty years of age under all the grease, grime and the deprivations of street life. Aurora has secreted a smoldering stick of incense in his clothes so that his

43

odor does not detract from the food, which is a tofu, green bean, sprouted live vegetation concoction.

"Would it hurt to cook us meat eaters a steak for once?" says Buster, ungratefully.

"You want meat, you cook it yourself – at your place, if you can find the kitchen that is," quips Aurora.

Tiffany turns to the homeless man.

"There's more, if you want it."

"Thanks."

"And a shower," adds Dwayne.

"Oh, no. Not in my shower," mutters Aurora. She smiles guiltily at the homeless man. "It's just that I don't have any change of clothes for you."

"Bound to be clothes that fit you in all the stuff we got at our place," says Buster.

"Appreciate it. Anything to drink?" asks the homeless man.

"Sure." Buster reaches down into a box near his feet and retrieving a wine-in-a-sponge packet.

"Cabernet Sauvignon, or Merlot?" asks the homeless person. Buster looks dumbfounded.

"Er, red, I think."

"I'll try it, thanks." Buster hands the homeless man a packet, which he opens then squeezes the wine into his glass.

"So let me get this straight, you went and got a mortgage for one year?" asks Tiffany as she pours homemade vinaigrette on her salad.

"Yup," replies Buster.

"And the contractor knows about this?"

"No, of course not. He probably presumes it's for twenty-five years," says Dwayne, "like most mortgages."

"We've got a contract from this Olaf guy that states that he'll pay the mortgage for the first six months. Didn't say how long the mortgage had to be, so we organized with the bank for a one-year mortgage and a two hundred and fifty grand loan."

"Won't that cause problems?" asks Tiffany.

"If it does, then it's his lookout," Buster says coldly.

"How did you come up with that crooked scheme?" asks Aurora.

"I closed my eyes and visualized abundance," he replies

sarcastically, "and I saw a big fat bank manager,"

"You never did tell us who this mystery investor is," she says, suspiciously.

Buster glances at Dwayne.

"Yeah, who is this Texan you told me about? I'd like to meet him," says Tiffany. "Perhaps he'd like to underwrite an expansion of our homeless shelters?"

"Well, he's some rich toff from Houston who wants to invest in businesses other than oil and doesn't travel to L.A. much."

"Was she one of the women that robbed the supermarket then?" asks Rachel in her sweet, high-pitched voice.

Buster looks at Rachel, confused and concerned by what seems like a non-sequitur.

"What supermarket's that Rachel?" asks Aurora.

"Oh, you wouldn't know about it, would you," interjects Tiffany. "It was on the TV. Just yesterday, two women robbed a Ron's Supermarket, the one we usually go to, and walked away with half a million dollars."

"As you know, we try and stay away from sour news. It gives off toxic vibrations," says Aurora.

"So does your cell phone," says Buster. "Don't see you givin' up that though, do I?"

"My business demands it. People need to get a hold of me," Aurora says defensively.

"You should get into fruit farmin', as you're a natural for cherry pickin'," gibes Buster. He looks to Rachel. "Anyway, this Texan investor is a man."

"So did *he* rob it then?" she asks.

"No, of course not."

"Did *you* rob it then?"

"Of course I didn't rob the supermarket." Buster dismisses the comment with a pathetic and somewhat guilty laugh.

"So, the half a million dollars in cash that was under the bed is not from the robbery?" asks Rachel.

Everyone stops eating. Buster freezes.

"There's money under the bed?" asks Tiffany.

"There was. Not so much now," says Rachel nonchalantly, as she eats. "It's just that yesterday it was the exact same amount of money that was robbed from the supermarket. I counted it when you were out."

Tiffany looks at Buster with disbelief.

"You robbed a supermarket?"

"You dressed up as women?" says Aurora gleefully.

"I never robbed a supermarket!" Buster insists. Everyone looks at him as if expecting an explanation. He puts down his cutlery. "Okay, okay. It's likely that the money under our bed was from the supermarket robbery. But I didn't steal it, *we* didn't steal it."

"Well, how did you get it then?"

"It fell from the sky on top of me," explains Dwayne.

"You found it?" asks Aurora looking at Dwayne.

"It found me. After our meetin', I needed to take an Eartha, so I got off the bike next to the road to do my business. That's where the sore bum came in. I think there was poison oak in the grass. Anyway, while I was there thinkin' about abundance, this bag of money lands on me." He looks to Buster. "And I thought it was because of *The Shhh*. Now you tell me it was a supermarket robbery?"

"Don't know for sure, but it looks like it," says Buster.

"So, how did the money come to land on Dwayne?" asks Tiffany.

"I guess it was probably thrown from the getaway car by the robbers," says Buster.

"But why would someone throw half a million dollars out of a car window?" asks Dwayne.

"How the hell do I know?"

"This wine is fruity, more like a Serat," interjects the homeless man, swirling the wine round in the glass. "No legs, though."

Everyone ignores him.

Dwayne looks a little hurt by the revelation.

"How come you didn't tell me? I'm your brother. We got no secrets."

"That's just it. You and this bloody *Shhh* thing. You live by it and I didn't want to burst your bubble, lettin' you know that it was nothin' but blind luck, a one in a million chance of you bein' where it landed."

"Not true. Dwayne believes in the power of *The Shhh* and that's why he attracted the money and it came to *him*." Aurora glares at Buster. "You don't and that's why you're a loser."

"What's this *Shhh* thing?" asks the homeless man.

"I'll get you a copy." Aurora touches the homeless man's arm and instantly regretting it.

"Technically, you're both guilty of receiving stolen goods," notes Rachel. "That's a federal crime."

Aurora throws down her napkin and gets up from the table.

"You take that money back you hear," she says, pointing towards the door. "I'm not having my Dwayne go to prison. Do you know how much processed food they serve in there? And I'm certain the soap isn't organic!"

"This is all your fault," says Buster to Aurora.

"My fault? And how do you figure that one?"

"If you hadn't kept feedin' him all this goat food and filled him full of fiber, he wouldn't have needed to relieve himself on the side of the road when the money landed on him."

Aurora is stunned into silence. Rachel, feeling guilty for starting an argument, looks to her mother for reassurance.

"My bad?"

"No dear," says Aurora.

"It's okay, Rachel. You did the right thing, sweetheart," acquiesces Buster, patting her long hair. "*We* did the wrong thing."

Aurora puts her hands on her hips in an authoritative manner.

"That's not your money. Take it back."

"I didn't steal it. It just hit me," says Dwayne.

"You didn't earn it, either."

"Over half of it's spent already, so we can't take it back," explains Buster.

"But it's not yours."

"Okay, I get it, *Janet*," snaps Buster. "Haven't you got a previous life to go back to or somethin'?"

"Buster, no need for that," chastises Tiffany. "Sit down, Aurora."

For once, Aurora does as she is asked.

"So instead of not lookin' this gift horse in the mouth, you want me to slap it on its arse and send it on its merry way, is that it?" asks Buster.

"Well, what *are* you going to do?" asks Tiffany.

"I was just goin' to keep quiet about it and do nothin'."

"But it's not *your* money, love. I thought you and Dwayne

were going straight?"

"I am. I didn't steal it, remember? We just kinda found it. I'll put all this right somehow, okay?" insists Buster. "And do we have to listen to those bloody bullfrogs on the sound system?"

Aurora cocks her head and looks at Buster.

"It's not on."

While Aurora and her guests are trying to locate the errant bullfrog in her living room, Carl and Greg are in *their* living room wondering how to find the mysterious man who took their bag of money. Or rather, Carl is the one brainstorming, while Greg is preoccupied by yet another zombie movie on the television.

Carl sits at the dining table in front of his old desktop computer, searching Google Earth and Google Maps. The Internet connection is slow and the noise from the zombie movie is distracting. Greg is so engrossed in the film that his hand, filled with popcorn, is frozen inches away from his open mouth.

"Got it!" Carl calls out.

Greg jumps in his seat, flicking popcorn everywhere.

"I think I know where this guy might be living," Carl says.

"What guy?"

"The guy that took our money, you dweeb!" Carl shakes his head. "Come here and I'll show you." Greg gets up. In just two strides, he is standing beside Carl. "Look. We were heading this way, right?" explains Carl, using his finger to point on the map on the computer screen. "You brilliantly threw the money out of the window here. That's where we first saw the guy. We know that he was heading this way, because we found the bike over here after the guy stole it off him."

"But we never found anyone with a bag when we looked in the mall."

"Well, I know that. He must have gone somewhere, either that or he was picked up by someone. But still, he was on a bike. Most people don't bike more than five miles, so I reckon with him cycling this way and a journey of five miles max, he was heading for Calabasas."

"That's still a big area. How we gonna find him?"

"Well, I got a quick look at him. He had dark hair, looked to be in his thirties, average build…"

"And a duffel bag of money!" says Greg.

"Well, he's not going to have that on him now, is he?"

"So, we just wander around Calabasas hoping to bump into this guy?"

"Considering we don't have jobs and we've got no money, I think that's exactly what we should do. We gotta think. What would an average Joe spend half a million bucks on?"

Buster, Tiffany, Rachel and the homeless man walk into Tiffany's cluttered apartment carrying plastic bags of groceries. Buster flicks on the light so he and the others can safely make their way along the narrow space between piles of furniture, books, clothes, ornaments, hat stands, baby supplies, ironing boards and anything else they could find for free on the Internet.

"And people accuse the homeless of hoarding junk," mutters the disheveled man.

"You'll find lots of clothes in there. Help yourself after you've had a shower," says Tiffany. She follows Buster past the cluttered kitchen to the short corridor that leads to the bedroom and bathroom.

"What are you doing with all this stuff?" asks the homeless man.

"Selling it on eBay," replies Tiffany with no enthusiasm.

"I can help you. I was in advertising before the crash. I could sell used chewing gum back to Wrigley in my day."

"That'd be great, thanks."

"Put all the stuff we just bought in the bedroom for now. It has the closest workin' fridge," says Buster, leading the group into the packed bedroom. He puts the groceries down and turns on the lights. "Let's put this where we can and nuke a real dinner with meat in it."

Tiffany sighs and drops her shoulders in despair.

"What love?" Buster asks.

"Can I please just get rid of this stuff and get our apartment back? We've been given more stuff that we can sell. I can't move in here anymore."

Buster thinks for a moment.

"I guess. See what you and your friend here can get for it all."

"No, Buster, I mean give it away. Most of it's junk anyway,

49

that's why other people were getting rid of it. I want it gone, so I can have a living room again and Rachel can have her own bedroom. So, if we have guests, they don't have to sleep in here with us."

Buster smiles back at her.

"Sure. With the pub goin' to start buildin' in the next day or two, we should be rollin' in it soon. Get rid of it all. Just keep some furniture, will ya? I might be able to use that in the pub."

"So, I can have my room back?" asks Rachel.

"Yes dear."

"Good. That means you two can have sex again," says Rachel.

# CHAPTER 4

As soon as the Wide boys hired Olaf as the contractor, construction on the pub commenced at a breakneck pace. Foundations have been poured, the timber frame erected, and the plumbing and wiring are nearly finished, albeit with many corners having being cut.

Rachel is off school and on summer break, dividing her time between playing with her friends and studying quantum physics at the local library.

Tiffany's apartment is back to normal with almost all the hoarded furniture and knick-knacks gone and the living room floor now visible for the first time in recent memory. Much of the furniture is in a storage unit, as Buster intends to use some of it in the new pub, thus saving a little money. The occasional homeless person, that the shelter cannot accommodate, still ends up spending the night on Tiffany's living room sofa, as her generous nature extends to those less fortunate than herself.

Unable to locate Dwayne or the money, Carl and Greg have been forced by Scott to take jobs at the same Ron's Supermarket that they robbed in order to pay him back. It is Scott's way of adding insult to injury and keeping an eye on them.

Aurora continues to sell her variation of spiritual awareness as a life coach, dismissing all modern conveniences, other than those that are convenient to her. She has a new bicycle that she has banned Dwayne from riding. He has taken to getting around on a one-speed bike that was part of the clutter being thrown out by Tiffany.

Leaning back in his chair, his fake alligator shoes resting on his desk, Olaf lazily glances out of the window. He is talking to a site manager via the Bluetooth in his ear. His black nylon wig is slightly askew, his shirt is now Barbadian rather than Hawaiian, but he continues to wear sunglasses even indoors.

"Do you have to truck soil away where you dug foundations? Can't you just dump it in back garden and say it is natural hill?" asks Olaf in his strong Slavic accent. "How about dump in neighbor's garden?" He listens. "Blame it on moles?" On the other end of the line, the site manager is irate. "Alright," says Olaf. "Just don't see point of spending money to get rid of something. Can we sell it?"

There is a gentle knock on the door. April, Olaf's secretary, walks in. She is wearing clothes that are so tight that they look like they have been put on underneath her skin. She is chewing gum, destroying the rumor that it is not possible for a California blonde to walk and chew gum at the same time. She silently hands Olaf the mail. He takes it and fixates his eyes on her backside as she leaves.

"Do we have another site where we can sell to them? That way, I charge on both ends." Olaf listens as he flicks through his mail. He opens the interesting ones. "I see." He skims a letter from the bank. Olaf quickly sits up and pulls his sunglasses off, revealing the raccoon patches around his eyes. "What the…?"

Buster, Dwayne and the construction foreman walk through the building site that will be the finished pub in less than two weeks. The construction crew, largely made up of Latinos, hammer, saw, measure and construct all around them. Drywall is starting to go up in several rooms. Dwayne has a clipboard and takes notes, as Buster pushes on an upright wooden strut to test strength and quality.

"Floorboards come in this afternoon, roof tiles first thing next week. After that it's internal cosmetics with paint, plaster and fixtures like the bar, toilets, sinks and the rest," says the foreman.

"Pop in some furniture, stock up the bar and the cellar then Bob's your aunty's live-in lover and we're open," says Buster with a smile. A worker with a newspaper walks by. "May I?" asks Buster. The worker nods and hands him the paper. Buster flips through the pages. The foreman looks to Dwayne with a quizzical look. "Ah!" exclaims Buster, as he hands the paper back to the worker.

"Good news?" asks the foreman.

"Yeah, I didn't win the lottery." Buster clenches a fist in victory. The foreman is confused, but lets it go. They proceed to the back of the construction site and emerge in the spot where a small bulldozer is clearing away an area of land.

"This is the back parking lot. It holds more cars than the front one and you just get to it from the side here. Asphalt should go down any day now."

There is a commotion behind them. All three turn to see an irate Olaf plowing through the construction site with a letter in his hand. Spotting his targets, he adjusts his wig and strides over to Dwayne and Buster.

"What the hell is this?" shouts Olaf as he reaches them.

"Looks like a letter to me," says Buster, sarcastically. "Does that look like a letter to you, Dwayne?"

"I believe it is."

"It more than letter. It bank statement!" Olaf's tanned, leathery skin is starting to perspire in the California heat. "Twenty thousand dollar a month mortgage? What the hell you playing at?"

"Just doin' what the contract says. I got a mortgage, you agreed to pay the first six months." Buster is gloating.

"Twenty thousand a month? I thought mortgage loan was for a quarter million?"

"It is."

Olaf strains to do the math, then it dawns on him.

"You got mortgage for one year?"

"Er....yup!"

Olaf stops and thinks for a moment.

"Clever. I like your style," he replies, calmer now and with a modicum of respect.

"Thank you."

"But this not legal." Olaf is angry again. "I not pay it. I *can't* pay it."

"You have to. We both signed the contract that you drew up," says Dwayne.

"But I can't. It ruin me."

"Then you default on the mortgage." Buster smiles smugly.

"Mortgage is in your name."

"Yeah, but you're on the hook for the first six months. You'll be in breach of contract, so I suggest you do somethin' about it, my little Russian friend." He looks at Olaf. "I know you skimmed thousands off the top of what we paid you. This is our insurance policy to make sure you finish properly. You do that, pay the first two months and we'll forget the rest."

"Two months!" cries out Olaf. "That forty thousand dollars!"

"I know. I reckon that's what you saved in shoddy workmanship and cheap labor."

Olaf looks outraged, although it is difficult to tell if his face is going red because of his deep tan.

"I'll finish this alright." Olaf turns and, cussing under his breath, walks back into the construction site.

The foreman returns to his work, leaving the brothers to look at the half-finished pub.

"What are we gonna name this place, anyway?" asks Buster.

The brothers stand in line at the checkout at Ron's Supermarket.

"The King's Head?" suggests Dwayne.

"Already got one," replies Buster.

"The Wide Receivers?"

"Too gay."

"The Dog's Bollocks?"

"Done."

"The Mutt's Nuts?"

"Get serious."

"Er, the British Pub?"

"Brilliant!"

"Yeah?" asks Dwayne excited.

"No!"

"The Wide Awake?"

"Better."

Dwayne looks around the supermarket.

"Hey, ain't this the store that was robbed?"

"Yup. That's what they call irony."

They reach the checkout that is manned by Greg, who starts to push groceries over the barcode scanner that *beeps* with every purchase.

"Did you find everything?" asks Greg in an automatic and bland fashion.

"Considerin' they're all stacked on shelves with product names on, I guess we did," replies Buster somewhat sarcastically.

"Twenty-three, fifty, please," says Greg in a monotone.

Buster and Dwayne pay up and leave.

Down one aisle of the supermarket, Scott wanders around pretending to check produce and being a manager. He is met by Lawanda, the store's customer service manager.

"Ah, Mr. Linus. It's good to see you back at work after your six weeks of *paid* leave." There is a less than subtle hint of sarcasm in her voice.

"Thank you. I can still see those guns pointing at me when I go to sleep at night, but I think being back at work is the best remedy."

"I'm sure it is." She leaves him to it.

He drops the façade and is about to go back to his office, when Carl walks in from the restroom area, tying up his apron.

"What are you doin' away from your counter?"

"Taking a pee."

Scott looks around to see if he will be overheard.

"Any luck finding my money?"

"It's *our* money, too, you know. We want it back as much as you do."

"It's going to take you a long time to pay me back working at your rate of pay."

"Yeah, and what are you going to do if we don't pay you back – report us to the police? I think they'd be really interested in knowing how you were involved."

Aurora sits in the lotus position on the floor of her living room, flanked by the bunny rabbit and the tortoise. The parrot looks down from a branch of one of the rubber plants. She balances her substantial bank account on her brand-new iPad.

"You need to find your center, locate that chakra, the third eye into your being," she is telling a client through the wired earpiece of her cell phone. When you've found that chakra, focus your life energy to a point where you can see nothing but that glowing chakra. Is it glowing?" The bunny rabbit sniffs at the iPad. "Uh-huh. I don't have you down as having ordered the chakra map. If you purchase the map, I'll be your GPS to guide you through the one-way streets to an energized life. Nineteen-ninety-five plus tax, two-day delivery."

The door opens and Dwayne walks inside. Aurora does not attempt to hide her electronic wares.

"I do need to move on to another appointment," she says. "Remember to book me before the prices go up next month, and I'm offering twenty percent off all healing work for two months if you bring me a new client." She waves at Dwayne as he takes off his shoes. "Gotta go. Bye." She hangs up. "There's a raw food wrap in the fridge."

"I'm not hungry, love." Dwayne walks across the room to kiss her.

"Chakra kiss, please," she instructs. Dwayne kisses her on the forehead. "That's better. Dare I ask how the pub is coming along?"

"Great, actually. We could be open for business in a week or so."

"That's a quick construction time."

"Yeah, well, cut a few corners here and there and save a day or two."

Dwayne heads to the bedroom. Once inside, he shuts the door, takes off his jacket, gets on his knees and quietly searches under the mattress for something. He is bemused when he cannot find it.

"Looking for this?"

Dwayne straightens up and turns to see Aurora standing in the doorway. She wears a pair of yellow rubber washing-up gloves and holds an open packet of beef jerky between a set of cooking tongs. He looks deflated, as if he has been caught with his hand in the cookie jar – especially if the cookies were not organic and the flour was processed.

"I'm not so much angry as I am disappointed," says Aurora. "I know this is Buster's influence on you, but I thought you were stronger than this." She holds up the beef jerky packet as if it were contaminated. "The dead, dehydrated flesh of bovine? It's not God's way."

"Then why did God have Noah herd animals onto the Ark and not vegetables, if we were supposed to be vegetarian?" he asks logically. "Unless he was gonna..."

"Don't go there," snaps Aurora cutting him off. "I only have your colon's best interest at heart, dear."

As soon as she has closed the door behind her, Dwayne smiles an inscrutable smile. He slides open a dresser drawer and reaches inside.

"I've got that one, too!" calls Aurora, from the other side of the door. Dwayne shuts the dresser drawer door, disappointed. He eagerly creeps to a sock drawer and rummages around. "And that one!" calls Aurora once again.

Dwayne gives up and sits dejected on the bed.

It is very early the next morning and well before any self-respecting cockerel would bother vocalizing the dawn of a new day. Buster is in bed, on his back, snoring as if he were inhaling the curtains. Tiffany sleeps soundly beside him, thanks to her industrial-strength earplugs.

On the nightstand, Buster's cell phone starts to ring the theme song of the old "Batman." TV show. In his sleepy state, he reaches over, picks up the TV remote and holds it to his ear.

"Yeah?" he says sleepily. "Speak up, I can't hear ya." After a moment, he realizes his error and scrambles to pick up his cell phone. "Yeah? Oh, hi Michael." Buster's eyes open wide. He sits up in bed as if fifty thousand volts had passed through him. "It's done what?"

Half an hour later, Buster, Dwayne and Michael stand with the foreman at the edge of the construction site. The pub, which is very nearly finished, has sunk six feet into the ground on its left edge.

Buster squints at the apparition with puckered lips, while Dwayne looks at it with his head cocked to one side.

"Is this what they mean when they say there's a lean on a house?" he says.

The foreman taps his mouth with a finger in thought.

"Looks like the entire foundation on the left side has collapsed. Could be subsidence."

"Or a cheap, penny-pinching contractor." Buster pulls his cell phone from his pocket and dials. "Where is he?"

Sitting in the waiting lounge at Los Angeles Airport, Olaf taps his fingers nervously on his knees as he looks around the busy terminal. He is wearing a gray jogging suit and a baseball cap, so as to look less conspicuous. His cell phone rings to the tune of *If I Were a Rich Man* from "Fiddler on the Roof." He looks at the caller ID and promptly turns it off.

Buster waits for Olaf's voicemail to engage.

"Hey, Olaf. It's your mate, Buster, here," he says with a fake smile and an ingratiating voice. "Now, I know we had a few words yesterday regardin' the mortgage thing, but I got a little situation that needs your attention relatin' to the pub construction. So, come on down to the site and we'll have a little chat, alright?" Buster hangs up and resumes his annoyed expression. He looks at Michael. "Nice recommendation."

"He was cheap."

"I can see why."

"What do we do now?" asks Dwayne.

"Going to cost a fortune to prop all that up," says the foreman.

"What did they do on the Batman set when this happened, Michael?" asks Dwayne.

"Gotham City didn't tilt like this, that was the camera."

"Well, we can't afford to go back, not with Olaf not payin' the mortgage and we're so close to completion. How much money is still in the kitty?" Buster asks the foreman.

"Enough for finishing the job, but not for anything like propping that up."

"So, does anyone have any bright ideas?" asks Dwayne.

A faint smile creeps over Buster's face.

"Yeah. We're goin' to make chicken salad out of chicken shit!"

Ten days later, a reluctant Aurora sits with her sister and Rachel in the back of the car with Buster at the wheel and Dwayne riding shotgun. It is a typical southern California summer morning, hot sunshine, cloudless skies and a trillion cars with only one person in each.

"Just look at all the pollution!" says Aurora.

"They now have cars powered by compressed air, you know. No fossil fuels, just compressed air that also turns an alternator for the battery, lights and radio."

"Not *hot* air?" asks Buster.

"No,"

"Pity. That way Aurora would be self-propelling," he says with a glance in his rearview mirror.

Aurora returns his look with a patronizing smirk.

"Horses. We should all go back to horses. Now that was how to get around. No pollution there,"

"Actually, Aunty Aurora," says Rachel, "the reason cars were invented was to alleviate the pollution from the manure that horses were leaving in the streets of the major cities like New York and London."

Aurora looks down at Rachel with disdain.

"Is there anything you don't know?"

"I won't know until I know it all, will I?" replies Rachel. "But probably."

Dwayne looks to the three girls in the back seat with a wide grin on his face.

"Hey, what goes clip…clop, clip…clop, clip…clop, BANG, clip-clop, clip-clop, clip-clop?"

"Dunno," says Tiffany.

"An Amish drive-by shooting."

Everyone except for Aurora bursts out laughing.

"And what do you call an Amish man with his hand up a horse's bottom?" No answers. "A mechanic!" Again everyone laughs.

Aurora manages a half-smile.

"How far is it to this place?" she asks.

"Almost there."

Ten minutes later, Dwayne pulls into the new parking lot of the pub. Everyone gets out of the car to get a good look at the boys' project.

In addition to the pub listing like a sinking ship, it now features windows that have been deliberately installed at helter-skelter angles and a front door that leans to the right in contrast to the foundation. Even the newly commissioned pub sign, The Tilting Tavern, hangs crooked.

"Ta-da!" announces Buster.

"I thought you fixed it?" asks Aurora, perplexed.

"This *is* fixed," explains Dwayne. "Fixed to be tilting. That's why we called it the Tilting Tavern."

"It's a hazard," Aurora complains.

"It's fun!" Rachel takes off in a trot towards the tilting front door. "Can we go inside?"

Buster unlocks the front door and they all walk in.

"Careful now, it's at quite a gradient. So watch how you walk around."

"The floor is distressed wood so that people's shoes have a better grip," Dwayne says, motioning for the ladies to enter first.

"I suppose it's the patrons who will be distressed when they see it – *if* they ever see it," mutters Aurora.

"So, this is where all our furniture from Craigslist went," says Tiffany, appraising the unmatched bookshelves, grandfather clocks and other household items that used to clutter her living room. The legs of the chairs and tables have been sawed off so they are at different heights and echo the feel of the entire pub.

"We can even use the breast pumps to pick up beer spills behind the bar," remarks Buster. "Waste not, want not."

"I love it!" Rachel says. "It's like a funhouse."

"Yeah, what's more fun than putting your beer down on a table and watching it slide to the floor?" Aurora mutters under her breath.

Buster ignores the dig.

"We turned a disaster into an asset. We purposely cut the doors and the windows to make it look even stranger."

"So, when you get drunk, it all levels out." Rachel runs her hand over the surfaces.

"Somethin' like that. Here, take a look at this."

Buster pulls a coin out of his pocket and balances it on its edge atop a table set at a steep angle. When he lets go, the coin appears to travel uphill. Rachel claps and jumps up and down, while Aurora feigns indifference.

"What other tricks have you got up your sleeve?" she asks.

"It's all aboveboard, so to speak."

"What's to say the other end won't collapse?" asks Tiffany, concerned.

"They did a good job on that end, it's just this end that's the problem. Builder says everything's okay," says Buster. "Toilets, office and other rooms are level though. It's just the main bar and the cellar that's all crooked."

Aurora stands in the middle of the bar with her hands on her hips looking around.

"Sorry, but who in their right mind would want to come here?"

Later that same evening, the Tilting Tavern car park is full of cars and the bar is packed with patrons. People are enjoying the strange room and all its quirky angles and odd furniture. Beer and wine flow freely, as does the money from patrons' hands.

Behind the packed, level bar, Buster and Dwayne are overwhelmed by the sheer number of customers seeking libations. A combination of music and loud voices make it difficult to hear what people are ordering.

"Yes, miss?" asks Buster loudly, leaning over the bar.

"Er, red wine. What have you got?" asks a young woman dressed up for the night.

"Merlot, Cabernet, Zinfandel or," Buster holds up a sachet, "wine in a sponge. Three bucks, all night. Very popular."

An overworked Tiffany is helping pick up empty glasses. She can hardly move for the packed patrons, all giggling and enjoying the bar's peculiarity. They have come from near and far, having seen or heard about this unusual pub and are now experiencing it for themselves. Just walking can be precarious, let alone with beers in hand.

Scott Linus, the Ron's Supermarket manager, is having a drink with friends. Buster recognizes Scott from the television interview, but does not let it show on his face. He just keeps a watchful eye on him.

Michael is regaling the crowd with stories of his early days as Batman. He hopes to meet a woman who shares Dwayne's gullible nature and take her home under the guise of being famous. This is Los Angeles, after all.

The under-age youth who stole the pink bike stands with a few of his friends, hitting on young ladies. When he sees Dwayne at the bar, he hides behind his friends and gets them to order his drinks.

In Aurora's apartment, candles are lit, incense is burning and sounds of a windy desert with chirping cicadas trip from the iPod speakers. On the bamboo-matted floor, surrounded by plants and animals alike, Rachel and Aurora assume the lotus position, facing each other. Aurora's eyes are closed. Rachel holds the white bunny to her chest and pets it. Scattered on the floor are chakra charts, meditation books and the DVD of *The Shhh*.

"Do you think bunny rabbits have an afterlife?" asks Rachel.

Aurora opens an eye, taken aback by the question.

"Er, yes, I suppose they do."

"And do you think that it's in some kind of heaven, like humans have a heaven?"

"I reckon it is."

"Do foxes and things like that also go to heaven?" presses Rachel, petting the rabbit.

"I think all animals do."

"So does the fox then eat the rabbit in animal heaven?"

"I doubt it. Then it wouldn't be heaven. It would be hell."

"Why not?"

"Because they're friends there."

"So, in heaven all animals are vegetarian?"

"I suspect they are," says Aurora, not sure where this is going.

"So, if God created everything including heaven, then why not make Earth like heaven so animals don't have to eat each other?"

"I'll ask God. Better still, you ask God," says Aurora smiling.

"Can't."

"Why not?"

"Because God doesn't exist," replies Rachel, very matter-of-fact. She puts down the bunny rabbit and picks up the tortoise. "I gave up all my imaginary friends when I turned six."

"You're nine, right?" Aurora asks. Rachel nods. "Don't you have nine-year-old friends you can play with?"

"They're either into Justin Bieber or Barbie. Same difference."

At two o'clock in the morning, the pub is closed and the patrons have gone. Buster and Dwayne are tired but happy with the first night of business. While an exhausted Tiffany cleans up the main bar, the two brothers huddle in the back office, counting the takings for the night. Buster drinks one of his wines in a sponge while Dwayne has a celebratory beer.

"Three thousand, four hundred and eighty two dollars," says Buster. He stretches his back and looks at the money on the table. "Not bad for a first night."

"And without selling food. We gotta get food."

"And a cook. We've got a small kitchen, so now we can use it."

"And a bar back," says Tiffany, as she staggers through the

door, wiping her hands on a tea towel. "I can't do anymore. I have to go to work tomorrow." She looks at her watch. "In six hours time!" Buster walks over to her and hugs her.

"We did good, girl. Three and a half grand," he says proudly.

"Good, you can hire an assistant." She pulls away and picks up her bag.

"And a bouncer," suggests Dwayne. "See some of the lowlifes we got in here? Didn't think Calabasas had people like that."

"You two live here," says Tiffany.

"True," replies Dwayne.

Buster picks up all the money and puts it in a small zip-lock bag.

"Right. Let's make like a shepherd and get the flock out of here."

# CHAPTER 5

A dejected Carl and a disheartened Greg return to their apartment in the evening after a hard day at the register of the Ron's Supermarket. Greg instantly turns on the television and looks for a zombie movie to watch, as Carl turns on his very old computer to check emails.

"I really don't think I can work there anymore," moans Carl. "That money was supposed to project us into a new life, not chain us to the old one." He looks at Greg. "All because some moron threw the money out of the window."

Greg ignores him and channel surfs, stopping on the news channel. On the screen, an attractive female reporter, holding a microphone, stands in front of the Tilting Tavern.

"Near the heart of downtown Calabasas, nestled amongst the shopping malls and tennis courts, sits a newly-constructed pub with a very unique look." The camera shows various recorded shots of the Tilting Tavern as the reporter continues her story. "A few weeks ago, this normal-looking pub was just another new building near completion. That was until the foundation on one side collapsed and sank into the ground by five feet. But did that deter the owners, two quick-thinking British brothers? Did they give up, knock it down and start all over again? I talked to them earlier today."

"Hey, Carl. Come take a look at this pub, will you?" Greg is happy to suspend his zombie movie quest in order to watch the news story. Carl cranes his body around and looks past Greg to the television. He is about to turn back to the computer when the image on screen changes to Buster and Dwayne being interviewed. Dwayne looks vaguely familiar to Carl, but he cannot think from where.

"So, what did you first think when you saw that your pub had collapsed?" asks the reporter.

"Well, we weren't happy," replies Buster. "My first reaction was to find the *BLEEEP*ing contractor and ask him what the *BLEEEP* he was doin' and why my *BLEEEP*ing pub was leaning over."

"We invested everythin' we have into this pub, so we was goin' to make sure that it was a success, tilting or not," adds Dwayne, who then smiles broadly into the camera.

Carl stares at the image of Dwayne, suddenly recognizing him as the person who found the duffle bag of money and cycled away with it. His eyes narrow in anger.

"So, instead of rebuildin' or proppin' up the foundations, we had this bright idea to keep it the way it was and make it into the Tilting Tavern," says Buster.

"These two talk funny," remarks Greg.

"Well, you know what they say," begins the reporter. "When life throws you lemons..." She holds the microphone to the brothers to finish the quote.

"It's easy-peesy, lemon-squeezy," says Dwayne.

Greg turns the channel, hoping to find a zombie movie.

"No. Put it back a sec," Carl commands. "I want to see where this place is."

Greg flips the channel back to the news.

"So, we turned what seemed like a disaster into an asset," says Buster. "All the doors, windows, paintings, fixtures, tables, chairs, everything have been changed to be wonky."

"You've only been open a few days. How's business?" asks the reporter.

"Booming." Dwayne is soaking up the camera. "Couldn't be better. The novelty aspect helps, but first and foremost we serve a great pint."

Buster holds up a sachet of wine.

"And wine-in-a-sponge. Just three bucks all night. Very popular."

"Any legal action against the builder for negligence?" asks the reporter.

Buster steps towards the camera threateningly.

"Yeah. When we find your *BLEEEP*ing sorry *BLEEP*, we'll *BLEEEP*ing well cut your..."

Dwayne stops him and pushes him back.

"What my brother is trying to say is that his mistake is our good fortune, one man's trash is another man's treacle. Know what I mean?"

The reporter turns away from Buster and Dwayne and smiles into the camera.

"So, there you have it. The Tilting Tavern here in Calabasas, open for business and taking a whole new *slant* on serving the customer."

The broadcast changes to the anchorman in the studio, pretending to be amused by her pun.

"Thank you, Maria. In fact, since our taping we've been able to track down the contractor, an Olaf Ashanov, who's in Mexico. Our correspondent in Cancun tried to talk to him."

The broadcast changes to show shaky, handheld images of Olaf, still heavily tanned, wearing sunglasses and a bright, gaudy, shirt. He now sports a blond wig in a pathetic attempt at a disguise.

"Me no speaky Engleesh. Me no comprehendo," says Olaf in a Russian version of a Mexican accent, as he hurriedly walks along trying to avoid being filmed. "You gotta da wrong crook. Me no hear of dem Wide boys." Olaf places his hand over the camera lens and the image reverts to the studio and the anchorman.

"In other news, earlier today in Glendale, police were called to the scene of an alleged goat molestation…"

"Perhaps we should take a look at this pub thing. Looks like a riot." suggests Greg. "So, can I watch my monster flick now?" When he gets no response, he turns to look at Carl, but he is nowhere to be seen.

In the small kitchen of the Tilting Tavern, the Hispanic chef, Jose, makes fast food appetizers to order. When an order for crab cakes comes in, he opens the frozen packet from the market, microwaves the cakes for two minutes, then crisps the tops with a blow torch that is usually reserved for crème brulée. Real crab cakes are outside of Jose's expertise: he used to work at Subway and is also a local gardener.

Another Hispanic employee dressed in white overalls slithers in between the customers collecting empty glasses and wiping down tables. It is another very busy night, the novelty of the tavern having spread like the rash that recently afflicted Dwayne's bottom.

Michael pushes his way to the front of the bar where Dwayne and Buster are serving. While neither brother is versed in the art of bartending, they are winging it as they both have done all their lives.

"Hey, Michael!" shouts Buster over the noise of patrons and the house music. "What'll it be?"

"Glass of your finest red again?"

"This one you pay for. Enough freebees."

"Hey, Buster, don't get cheap on me. Who got you this land at a discount price?"

"And who paid you in cash for your services?"

"Shh!" hisses Michael looking around.

"Alright," replies Buster. "But this is the last time. After tonight, you pay for your drinks like all the other punters."

"Deal. In that case make it a double wine."

Buster smiles.

"I got the best stuff out the back. Give me a moment." Buster turns to Dwayne. "Back in a bit."

"What? Don't leave me here alone," protests Dwayne, gesturing towards the crowd of people three deep at the bar.

"Michael, help Dwayne while I'm gone." Buster steps out from behind the bar and motions for Michael to take his place.

"Alright." Michael puffs out his chest. "Did a bit of this when I was young." He turns to three girls that overhear the conversation. "When I was at Lee Strasburg in New York, that is."

Inside the kitchen, the noise from the bar is greatly diminished. Jose is opening a new packet of frozen spanakopita when Buster walks in.

"Hey, Jose."

"Señor Wide."

Buster takes a wine glass from a box of extra ones and places it on the table. He then pulls a couple of sachets of wine in a sponge from another box.

A very expensive, chauffeur-driven Bentley glides smoothly into the front parking lot of the Tilting Tavern. It is impossible to park, so the car just stops outside the entrance and a man in a business suit steps out. He looks as though he would be more comfortable at a legal bar than a drinking one. He has short gray hair, thinning on top, a little portly in frame, but with the stature of someone important. He gives instructions to his chauffeur and walks towards the entrance.

At the same time, Buster returns to the noisy bar with a very full glass of wine in his hand.

"Here you go," he says, handing it to Michael. "Mendecino two thousand and two."

"Ah, thanks." Michael steps out from behind the bar so that Buster can resume his post. He sips the wine. "Nothing like the Napa Valley shiraz." He holds up his glass in thanks and makes his way back into the throng of customers.

"And that ain't nothing like a Napa Valley shiraz, neither," Buster mutters to Dwayne. He turns his attention to the mature man in the business suit who has managed to belly up to the bar. "Yes, Guv, what can I get ya?"

"Gin and tonic, please," shouts the businessman. "Better make that a large one, as I don't think I'll be able to make it back to the bar again."

"You got it." Buster turns to make the drink.

"Is it always this busy?"

"Dunno. Only been open a few days."

"Is this typical for a British pub?"

"No, nobody's started fighting yet," Buster shouts over the din of the bar.

"Well, it's a very unusual place you have here – quite unique. More interesting than mine."

Buster finishes making the drink.

"Oh, yeah? You got a pub then?"

"Several hundred, actually."

"Several hundred?" Buster pushes the drink to him.

The businessman places his card on the bar.

"Chuck Patton. I'm the CFO for Brenton Brewery. Head office is up in Santa Barbara. We own breweries, hotels and a chain of supermarkets like Ron's. You may have heard of us?"

"Of course. Could say I've done business with you."

"Brenton Brewery is always interested in adding another pub to its list."

"It's a bit early to sell up. I've only been open a few days. And as you can see, I've got a tidy little crowd."

A tall man next to the businessman is getting impatient that he has not yet been served.

"Hey, do you give free beers if it's someone's birthday?" he shouts.

"Why, is it your birthday?"

"I've had two while waiting to get served!"

"Very funny. Whadda-ya-want?"

"Three beers and two glasses of sweet white."

"Right." Buster turns to get the beers.

"I'll make you a very attractive offer," shouts out Mr. Patton. "How does one million sound?"

"Tempting, but nowhere near enough." Buster lines up the glasses for the wine. "Land alone's worth half that."

Mr. Patton pulls out his wallet to pay.

"On the house, mate," says Buster pushing Mr. Patton's money back at him.

"Why does he get a free drink?" moans the tall man.

"It's his birthday," replies Buster with a winning grin.

Mr. Patton takes back his money.

"You should take the offer while you can. There's a reason my company owns hundreds of pubs."

"If I sell, I'll add the drink to the bill." Buster thinks on his feet. "Oh, try this revolutionary idea of mine," he says, reaching back and retrieving a sachet. "Wine-in-a-sponge. Catch on like the plague."

Mr. Patton smiles, takes the drink and the sachet, and walks away. Buster pockets his card before turning his attention to the impatient customer.

As Mr. Patton tries to find a quieter corner and deal with the weird angles and tilts of the bar, he is spotted by Scott. He then sees Carl, battling through the crowds. Scott hides himself from view behind the people he is talking to. He eagerly watches Carl, hoping that he will not be seen.

Carl is totally taken aback by the tilting floor, odd angled windows and furniture. He bumps into the under-age youth that he and Greg forced off the stolen bike thinking it was Dwayne.

"Excuse me," says Carl as he tries to pass. They give each

other a look, as if they should somehow recognize each other. Carl breaks the stare, turns his attention to the bar where Dwayne and Buster are serving customers.

After a few minutes of patiently waiting, Carl makes it to the bar.

"Yes, mate?" Dwayne says to his bald, diminutive customer.

"Lager, draft."

"You got it." Dwayne draws a pint.

"Nice place you got here. Just saw you on the news."

"Yeah, didn't get me good side though, did they?" laughs Dwayne.

"This place must have cost a pretty penny?"

"Not as much as you'd think." Dwayne finishes pouring.

"Didn't get much change out of that half a million, then?"

Dwayne places the pint on the counter and looks at Carl's humorless expression.

Five minutes later, Carl stands in the back parking lot, with the pint in his hand, waiting. Buster and Dwayne emerge from the pub's back door.

"Alright, wadda ya want?" Buster wipes his hands on a bar towel and stares down Carl.

"My money back," says Carl.

"Don't know what you mean, mate."

"Let's not play games. I recognize this guy from the roadside. You took the money, *my* money."

"It's not *yours*. You stole it from that supermarket," says Dwayne.

"And you stole it from me."

"That's where you're wrong. Technically, you gave it away."

"I was temporarily relocating it when you happened upon it," argues Carl.

"Do you really expect us to give it back?" says Buster. "And how? It's all spent on this pub."

"Not my problem. If you don't give me my money, I tell the cops."

"And we'll tell on you. We just found the money, we didn't steal it."

"I can't be linked to the robbery. That's how I planned it. No finger prints, no hair." He then remembers that he is bald. "I bet you'd find it very difficult to prove where half a million dollars came from in cash to buy this place."

Buster glances at Dwayne, then back to Carl.

"So, what are you proposing?" he asks.

"Seeing as how you can't give the money back, you'll have to cut me in on the deal. Make me a partner in the pub."

"And if we don't?"

"I'll make it difficult for you to stay open."

"What, you and the other six dwarfs?" chuckles Dwayne.

"No need to get personal. Not my fault I'm vertically challenged."

"Sorry, mate." Dwayne looks away sheepishly.

"Look, get lost. Go away. Don't bother us again," orders Buster as he storms off towards the pub's back door.

"I'm not kidding. I'll go to the cops!" calls out Carl.

Buster continues walking away leaving Dwayne with Carl. There is a long silence.

"What is it?" asks Carl.

"That's three-bucks-fifty for the pint."

"Oh, right, sorry." Carl reaches into his pocket and pulls out a five-dollar bill. "Can I get all the change in quarters? I've got laundry tomorrow."

Dwayne fumbles in his pocket.

"Yeah, should be able to." He hands over some change. "There you go."

"Thanks."

Dwayne smiles at Carl until he remembers why he is there. His features turn sour.

"Now clear off!"

Suspicious of anyone that his ex-partners-in-crime may meet, Scott Linus has been observing everything from behind a parked car.

Buster and Dwayne are back behind the bar serving customers when Dwayne spots Carl's bald head bobbing in between the scrum of customers fighting for prime bar real estate.

"Excuse me, excuse me, please!" he says.

"Now what?" snaps Dwayne, once Carl has made it to the bar.

Carl holds up the ends of a car battery jumper cable.

"Can you jump me?"

# CHAPTER 6

Tiffany's living room has been free of Craigslist clutter for some time. It now looks like a normal living room with a sofa, chairs, carpets, a flat-screen television, DVD player and, unlike her sister's indoor rainforest set-up, just one plant – a plastic one.

Buster, Dwayne and Tiffany sit around the dining room table in front of a dozen or more open potato chip packets and a large bowl. They each take a chip, examine it and either place it in the bowl, or eat it.

In the kitchen, off the living room, a homeless woman helps Rachel open sachet after sachet of wine-in-a-sponge and squeeze the contents down funnels into empty bottles of expensive Napa Valley wine.

"Make sure you don't lick the drops off your hands, Rachel," Tiffany says from the living room. "This isn't fruit juice and I don't want a tipsy nine-year-old on my hands."

"I know," says Rachel. "It's the product of fermented grapes converting fruit sugars into alcohol and carbon dioxide."

"Good girl."

Rachel glances over to see what they are doing.

"Why do you have all those potato chip packets open? Is there going to be a party?"

"No, love. Buster is convinced that this is going to be a big money earner," replies Tiffany.

"Potato chips? How?"

"Well, Rachel," explains Buster, "you may have seen it on the news, you know, someone who thinks they saw the face of Jesus or the Virgin Mary on a grilled cheese sandwich or on a stained T-shirt and thinks it's a miracle. Then some rich geezer or Jesus-freak buys the sandwich for twenty grand because he thinks it's a sign from God."

"Why would anyone buy something like that?" asks Rachel.

"Never underestimate the stupidity of people, dear," says Tiffany.

"So, we're gonna give them a miracle in the form of a potato chip, or crisp, as we Brits call them."

"So, each day we'll open several packets and see who's in there and what we can put up on eBay."

Dwayne holds up a chip.

"Does this look like Richard Harris or Glenn Close?" he asks.

"I thought Richard Harris *was* Glenn Close," says Buster.

Tiffany leans over and looks at the chip.

"Looks more like George Bush senior, I think."

Buster pops the chip into his mouth, disappointed.

Tiffany picks up another chip and looks at it excitedly.

"Look, Elvis," she proclaims. She turns it over and back again. "Presley, Costello, Presley, Costello. Two for one."

"In the bowl it goes. How many's that?" asks Buster.

Tiffany looks into the bowl.

"Er, one."

Buster looks fed up with eating all the crisp rejects.

"This is worse than mining diamonds. At least with diamonds you don't have to eat the dirt you're sifting through."

"And you can make how much on one of these again?" asks Tiffany.

"The sky's the limit. There was once a piece of bread that looked like the Pope that went for just over twelve grand."

"For a piece of bread?" Tiffany raises an eyebrow.

"It's always the religious nuts. They've got more money than incense. Ha! Get it, incense?"

Tiffany smiles indulgently, then searches for another high-value chip.

Buster's cell phone rings. He answers it.

"Hey, Michael, what's up?" Buster listens for a moment, then freezes. "He did *what*?"

Twenty minutes later, Buster and Dwayne are sitting on the sofa in Michael's rather splendid house. They are looking at official city forms spread out on the coffee table.

"How can our building permits be no good, now?" asks Buster.

"The pub's built. Okay, it's tilting, but it's built."

"Well, the permits were good while my brother-in-law was working in the permit office," says Michael, emerging from his tricked-out kitchen and wiping his hands on his Williams-Sonoma apron. "Now that he's been arrested for issuing fraudulent permits, local government is investigating everything he issued in the last three years."

"What does that mean for us? Are we in trouble?" asks Dwayne.

"Probably. And the pub will likely have to shut down," explains Michael, as he walks back into the kitchen. "Especially with the subsidence. He was able to do a cover-up on that one with more dodgy permits before he got nabbed. That pub isn't safe, you know."

"It's perfectly safe, for a building that's listing to one side. Look at the Leaning Tower of Pizza," adds Buster. "Nobody's being stopped from going up that."

Michael walks over with a plate of cupcakes straight from the oven. He sits down opposite the brothers.

"Cupcake, anyone?" he asks, setting the plate down on the coffee table. "I made them myself."

"Are they made with organically grown grain and purified water, no dairy, with ingredients that haven't been exposed to pesticides, and were picked by workers earning more than minimum wage?"

Michael looks bemused.

"No."

"Thank God!" Dwayne grabs a cupcake and consuming it voraciously.

Buster's mind is still locked on the problem.

"But we've only been open a short time and business is great. We're making bank. We can't close now. So what do we do?"

"Let me think." Michael stands and paces around the living room in his socked feet.

"But we didn't do anything wrong," moans Dwayne through a mouthful of crumbs.

"Technically, you did. You paid for expedited permits that my brother-in-law provided."

"But you took care of it, not us."

"With your money."

"Ah, but the money's not ours, it was stolen!" Dwayne says with gusto before realizing that he should have kept his mouth shut.

Buster shakes his head, marveling at his brother's stupidity.

"I've been spending stolen money?" asks Michael, stopping in his tracks.

"We didn't steal it."

"It fell on me at the side of the road," explains Dwayne.

"It did what?" Michael looks between Buster and Dwayne as the penny drops. "You two robbed that supermarket? So that's how you got the money by the next day!"

"No, we didn't."

"Disguised as women. Very clever."

"We didn't rob any supermarket!" insists Buster, loudly.

"The money came to me because of *The Shhh*."

Michael looks at Dwayne.

"You've seen *The Shhh*?"

"Read the book. Not allowed to see the DVD."

"Oh, the DVD is great."

"How's it workin' for you?"

"Weeeell." Michael tilts his outstretched hand in a 'so-so' gesture.

"Hasn't got you any more Hollywood jobs, then?"

"Lads!" interrupts Buster. "Focus. Wadda we gonna do?"

"Who else knows that your pub was bought with stolen money?" asks Michael.

"Our girlfriends and Rachel, my bird's daughter," says Buster. "So, what are we going to do?"

Michael starts pacing again, hand to chin, deep in thought.

"There's still the reward."

"Reward? Reward for what?" asks Dwayne, ears pricked.

"Well, there has to be a reward for the return of the money," says Michael. "Especially that much. That's what normally happens in situations like this."

"How much?" asks Buster.

"Ten percent, I guess. Fifty grand."

"Well, we've met one of the robbers already," says Buster very matter-of-factly.

"You have? Where?"

"He came into the pub last night demanding his money back. Nice guy. Funny-looking. Wanted me to jump him," says Dwayne. "He saw us on TV, so that's how he knew to find us."

"Yeah, I saw that, too," says Michael. "You looked good."

"Thanks, but it wasn't my best side," says Dwayne, flattered.

"This isn't helping," snaps Buster. "We need a plan."

Michael paces the room again.

"Let me think for a minute."

"Well, hurry up. We gotta open the pub shortly," says Buster.

"Can I have another fairy cake?" asks Dwayne.

Buster sits back, throwing his arms up in frustration.

"Ah!" cries Michael.

Buster and Dwayne lean in.

"You got an idea?"

Michael looks down at one socked foot.

"No. I stepped on a staple."

Buster, with Dwayne riding shotgun, pulls into the Tilting Tavern parking lot and finds a space. Buster notices Carl's beat-up 1976 VW van as he parks. He and Dwayne get out and start to walk to the front door of the pub. Carl and Greg emerge from behind the VW van.

"Oh God, not you again," groans Buster. "Who's the stick insect?"

"You're right, they are rude," says Greg to Carl.

"Are you brothers, as well?" asks Dwayne in all seriousness. Carl looks up to Greg, as Greg looks down on Carl. There is at least a foot difference in height.

"No, this is my partner in crime, metaphysically and literally," says Carl.

"Hi-ya," says Greg with a big grin. "I'm Greg."

"Bit careless with your money ain't ya, sweetheart," mocks Buster.

Carl wears a serious expression.

"We're in on this Tavern whether you like it or not. It's our money. We stole it, then you stole it from us. That makes us partners."

"Or else," begins Greg. He is outwardly stoic and composed,

but on the inside he's a timid mouse squeaking with trepidation. "We can make an anonymous call. You don't know who we are or where we live. But I'm sure that the police and the supermarket owners will be very interested in talking to *you*."

"If we're not going to keep the money, then you're not either," says Carl.

Buster nods to Dwayne and they step to one side. Buster whispers gibberish in Dwayne's ear.

"Schwub-geerfle-bladdan-crusbel-shwibber-wibber. Fleel-y-k-sheer-seer-verlerble."

Buster turns and stares at Carl and Greg with a smug look of superiority on his face.

Dwayne looks very confused.

"I didn't understand a word of that," says Dwayne. Buster leans in and whispers more gibberish in his ear, before standing and looking threateningly at Carl and Greg. "Nope. Didn't get that either," mutters Dwayne.

"I'm trying to make it look like I'm whispering something important in your ear, to scare them," says Buster, louder this time. "But I already know what I want to say, so I don't really need to say it to you. That's why I'm talking gibberish. Get it?"

"Oh, I get it," says Dwayne nodding. He then leans in and offers him his ear. "Carry on, then."

Buster is about to lean in when he stops himself.

"Well, there's no point now is there? They know what I'm trying to do."

Carl and Greg just look to each other, confused by it all.

Buster steps closer to the two Americans.

"I tell you what. You two come and work with us as barmen…"

"Managers," corrects Carl.

"Whatever, and we'll see how it goes. I don't want a couple of tea leaves workin' behind my bar unless I can trust them," says Buster. "Come on in and I'll show you boys how we operate. If you work out, you can do some of the late shifts and give us a few nights off. Might as well get somethin' out of this." Buster leads Carl to the front door. "I hope you're more careful with the till takings than you were with the supermarket money. Dress code is smart casual and preferably men's clothing, okay?"

A couple of days later, Tiffany is preparing to serve dinner in her kitchen, while Buster, Dwayne, Aurora, Rachel and an elderly homeless man sit at the table in the living room waiting to be served. The enticing aroma of cooked food waft from the kitchen into the living room, even sending Aurora's olfactory senses into overdrive, although she hides it very well.

At the table, Rachel is reading "War and Peace," while Dwayne tackles another crossword puzzle. Buster picks up a bottle of Napa Valley wine.

"Wine, Aurora?" he asks.

"About what?" is her reply.

"No, do you want some wine? Label says Merlot from the Napa Valley and four-years-old."

"I don't think so."

"Look, you're here at our place now. We cook food and we drink wine. Nobody's going to judge you. You make us eat rabbit food at your place, so let your hair down and be one of us for a change."

She considers his request.

"Napa Valley, you say?"

"That's what the label says." Buster glances at Dwayne.

"Oh, alright then. Just a small one. I'll say when." Buster pours her a glass, and keeps pouring, waiting for her to say when. Only as the wine gets to the top of the glass and is almost full, does she call out, "When." Buster puts the bottle down. Aurora takes a big sip. "What's this I hear about you selling potato chips on the Internet?"

"Yeah, we got a great one of the Pope, looks just like him."

"Which one?"

"Dunno. They all look the same, if you ask me."

"Got a few others, as well. One is Marty Feldman, that or it's just an ugly chip, and the third is Karen Carpenter, but only if you turn it sideways."

"And how are they doing?"

"Initial bids on the Pope are over three grand."

"For a potato chip?" exclaims Aurora. "And I thought I was a..." She stops herself from further incrimination and sips her wine.

"Buster thinks we could get ten grand for that one alone," says

Dwayne, not even looking up.

"So, it's another con, right?" says Aurora.

"Nothin' crooked about this venture," insists Buster. "All above-board. Just tappin' into the unique market of superstitious idiots."

"Ever thought of getting a proper job?"

"Have you?" retorts Buster, glowering at her. Aurora looks over to Dwayne.

"Dare I ask what's going on with the pub?"

Dwayne puts down his crossword puzzle.

"I told you, dear, that we're up to our eyeballs in buildin' permit issues. The city may shut us down. Michael is stallin' them until he knows what's goin' on."

"Plus, that builder's done a bunk, leavin' us to pay the crazy one-year mortgage that we can't afford, as we've spent all the money," adds Buster.

"That little stunt came round to bite you in the butt, didn't it?" says Aurora with a smirk.

"The pub's doin' really well, but if we don't want to default and take on the enormous mortgage payments, then there's literally nothin' to live on."

"Hence, the chip venture," says Tiffany from the kitchen, where she has been following the conversation. "Dinner's ready in a minute."

"I could change the mortgage back to twenty-five years and have much lower payments."

"Property taxes," mutters the homeless man.

"Do what?"

"Property taxes," repeats Rachel as she looks up from the book. "He's right. You forgot the one-point-five percent property taxes, half of it due every six months. That's about seven and a half thousand every six months."

The homeless man smiles.

"I was a mortgage broker once."

"If things are so tight, why are you hiring new staff?" asks Aurora. "You know, the short bald one and the tall, gangly one?"

Buster glances at Dwayne.

"Carl and Greg? Oh, they're just people we know who can give us a night or two off, like tonight."

"I hope you can trust them."

"They've got an interest in seein' that the pub does well," remarks Dwayne.

"It's times like these that not playing the lottery to save money sounds like rational thinking," says Aurora. "Don't suppose you've accidentally won, have you?"

"Nope," replies Buster, gleefully.

Tiffany walks to the table and places the hot plates of food in front of Aurora and Dwayne.

"Put the book down now, Rachel love. Dinner's ready," says Tiffany.

Aurora is feeling the effects of having taken a couple of large gulps of wine on an empty stomach.

"What are we having?" she asks.

"You're having vegetarian, sorry, *vegan* lasagna and we're having ordinary beef lasagna," says Tiffany on her way back to the kitchen.

"Different serving utensils, right?" calls out her sister, somewhat paranoid.

"Of course." Tiffany returns and places the remaining plates before her guests then sits. They are about to start eating when Aurora puts her hands out.

"A blessing. Dwayne."

Aurora extends her hands further and more insistently. The others reluctantly do likewise, including the elderly homeless man.

Dwayne thinks for a moment.

"Look out stomach, look out tongue, it ain't staying long 'til it's out your bum," he says solemnly.

Aurora is not amused, but Rachel and the elderly homeless man laugh.

"Well, tuck in," instructs Tiffany.

The lasagna on each of the plates looks as appetizing as it smells.

The elderly homeless man begins to devour his voraciously.

"This is wonderful, thank you," he says to Tiffany.

"You're welcome, sweetie. Plenty more."

"This tastes terrific," adds Dwayne. "Never knew veggie food could be this good."

Buster appears less impressed with his, but says nothing.

Aurora takes small bites of her food, but does not want to show anyone that she is really enjoying a cooked meal for the first time in ages. She holds her stoic expression but, inside, her salivary glands are doing the rumba with her tongue.

"Um, nice," she says with characteristic understatement. "I'm impressed, little sister."

"You used to love mom's cooked food, before you got all tree-huggy," recalls Tiffany, enjoying her own cooking.

"So, how *are* you going to resolve the problems with the pub, Buster?" asks Aurora with her mouth half-full.

"Hmm," he says, thinking as he swallows. "Michael says that if the city finds out that we were involved in the permit fraud, then there are heavy fines to pay and the pub will have to shut down until the permits are issued legally."

"Which might mean having to either prop the pub up so it's flat, or demolish it and lose everything," adds Dwayne.

"And get lumbered with the quarter-million mortgage to pay back," says Buster. "We can't afford to stay open and we can't afford to close."

Aurora looks to Rachel.

"See, Rachel. This is what happens when you try to do things the wrong way."

"She'd never do that anyway, would you dear?" says Tiffany.

"No. I'd have opened up a limited liability company with only ten thousand dollars in assets, so if I was sued, I couldn't be touched personally."

The adults look to each other, then back at Rachel.

"Why didn't you tell us to do that in the first place?" asks Buster.

"You never asked. Also, I think I was at gymnastics that day."

"Okay, clever pants, what would you do now?" asks Dwayne, thinking he has the better of her.

"I'd sell for one million minimum, give back the two hundred and fifty thousand to the bank, give back the half million to the supermarket and pocket the remaining two hundred and fifty thousand. Capital gains on the profit is a hundred thousand so you'll be left with a hundred and fifty thousand to split between the two of you." Rachel goes back to eating.

"I concur," adds the homeless guest.

Buster looks befuddled.

"Why give back the half million to the supermarket?" Everyone around the table give him a 'are you kidding?' look. "Okay, okay. But surely the novelty value of the pub makes it worth more than a million?"

"Not in this down market and certainly not with the permit issues," says Rachel. "The longer you wait, the more likely you are to be stuck with it. I'd sell as soon as possible and start again somewhere else."

Dwayne looks demoralized.

"Sell, but to who? We don't know anyone who would buy it as is?"

Buster smiles to himself and says nothing.

"This is really good, Mom," says Rachel.

"Aw, thank you, love."

"Yes, it's quite good, Tiffany," concedes Aurora.

"Yeah, very tasty," says Dwayne, happy to be eating a hot cooked meal for once.

Buster still looks unimpressed.

"Mine's a little bland, to be honest."

"So's mine." Tiffany reaches over and tastes Aurora's dinner. She then takes a bite off of Dwayne's plate. "Oh, silly me, I wondered if I got them the wrong way round." Embarrassed, she swaps Dwayne's with Buster, then switches her plate with a horrified Aurora. "Oops, sorry."

# CHAPTER 7

Due to its overwhelming popularity, the Tilting Tavern is now open from midday to two in the morning and business is booming.

It is a relatively quiet early afternoon, and Dwayne is out in the lounge area chatting with the patrons, while Buster is behind the bar. Customers are still enjoying the odd-angled tables and furniture and the purposefully slanted front door and windows. Surprisingly, there have been very few accidents. Simon and Garfunkel's song *Slip Sliding Away* is appropriately playing over the speakers.

Buster looks up from cleaning a glass to see Mr. Patton and a burly-looking chauffeur, probably his bodyguard, walk inside. The chauffeur is taken unawares by the slanting floor and nearly falls, much to the amusement of those already in the bar. It is almost a rite of passage.

"Mr. Wide," says Patton in greeting, as he and his chauffeur saunter up to the bar. "Nice midday crowd you got here."

"Ah, Mr. Patton. Yeah, yeah, all tickin' along quite nicely, thank you. Nights are madness, as you can imagine. Got my message, I take it?" Buster asks with a confident smile.

"Indeed. That's why I'm here. Do you have a few minutes, somewhere quiet?"

Buster leads them back to a small office area beside the kitchen. Unlike the rest of the bar, this room is level. The chauffeur closes the door behind them.

Mr. Patton silently hands Buster some papers.

"I took out a patent on the concept and design of this bar or any bar that is tilt-themed," he says. "You are now in violation of my patent." Buster looks at the papers, totally bewildered. "You're either going to have to pull this bar down and build a straight, normal-looking one, or sell to me. What's it going to be?"

Buster looks stone-faced, but on the inside is dancing a jig. He sighs deeply and shakes his head.

"Looks like you got me done up like a kipper, Mr. Patton."

He has no idea what Buster is talking about, although it sounds like the words of a defeated man.

"Oh, and by the way, the price has dropped to seven-hundred-and-fifty thousand," adds Patton with a smile of satisfaction.

"What? That means I walk away with nothin' at all!" protests Buster, genuinely shocked.

"Welcome to the business world, Mr. Wide." He places a contract and pen on the table. "Sign this. Cash sale, just like buying a car. I want you and your staff out within the hour. I got my own people outside in a van. We'll take on all the inventory and assume the bills as part payment." He takes one step closer to Buster. "I'm not greedy, keep what's in the registers."

Mr. Patton raises a hand and clicks his fingers. The burly chauffeur retrieves a ten-dollar note from his pocket and hands it to Mr. Patton, who drops it on the table. "That's for the drink the other night. Keep the change."

In his living room, which is illuminated only by the flickering light of the TV, Greg is stretched out on the sofa as though he were a rack victim of the Spanish Inquisition. Although it is daytime, the curtains are drawn. Greg watches another zombie film, this time one from the 1960s, of poor quality and badly acted. Even so, he is engrossed in the action, mechanically shoveling M&Ms from a packet into his mouth.

Someone parts the curtains all of a sudden.

"Ah!" cries Greg, sitting up in fright, scattering M&Ms everywhere.

"We've gotta be at the pub in an hour," says Carl. "So, take a shower and get ready."

"I had one yesterday!" Greg protests.

"Suit yourself." Carl retreats to the bathroom. There is a knock at the door. "Get that, will you?" Carl calls through the closed door.

Greg lethargically opens the door, while keeping an eye on the television.

"Is stupid in?" asks Scott, standing in the doorway.

Greg looks confused.

"Which one of us is that?"

Scott pushes past him into the room. Greg closes the door behind him.

"Hey, Einstein? Where are you?" calls out Scott.

Carl emerges from the bathroom with toothbrush I hand and foam around his mouth.

"We don't work for you anymore, so don't start on us," says Carl, looking like a rabid dog.

"You can't quit the supermarket when you owe me quarter of a million big ones," snaps Scott, standing with his hands on his hips.

"Get over it," says Carl, spitting toothpaste foam as he speaks. "It's not going to appear out of thin air."

"Really? Why not?" asks Scott sarcastically. "That's where you threw it."

Greg looks at Carl and then back at the television. Onscreen, a zombie who is frothing at the mouth, is attacking a beautiful actress.

"We don't have it and..."

"Working at that Tilting Tavern pub, I see," interrupts Scott.

"What if we are?" asks Greg, trying to keep an eye on the television.

"Got a little something going with the owners of that pub, haven't you?"

"Got a better job, that's all," retorts Carl.

"I bet you have, I bet you have." He looks from Carl to Greg. "Wouldn't happen to have bought that pub with any ill-gotten gains, would they by any chance?"

Buster and Dwayne walk up the stairs to Tiffany's apartment, half-elated that the Tilting Tavern is off their hands, but disappointed that there is no money in it for them except for the few dollars from the cash registers.

"Seven-hundred-and-fifty grand sitting in the bank and we can't touch any of it," moans Buster.

"Whadda we gonna do now?" asks Dwayne.

"Focus on the chip income. See what that brings us. That and the reward we're gonna get for finding the money, which technically you did."

"You could actually try winning the lottery."

"Why? Having not lost two grand over the last four years pretty much tells me that what I'm doin' is workin'."

"If you used the power of *The Shhh*, you'd win it one day."

"You and I need to have a chat about that. What happened to the duckin' and divin', wheelin' and dealin' pessimistic brother I used to know? Ever since you moved in with off-the-planet-Janet, you've changed."

They reach the top of the stairs leading to Tiffany's front door.

"I want a word with you," comes a voice from along the corridor.

Buster and Dwayne see Scott walking towards them, flanked by Carl and Greg, each holding a wrench in their hands.

"You've got something of mine and I want it back," adds Scott.

Buster stands his ground, defiantly.

"You're the supermarket manager, right? I saw you on the TV, then at the pub the other night." Buster hesitates. The penny drops. "So, you three are..? Oh, it all makes sense now."

"What does?" asks Dwayne, a few brain cells behind the current thinking.

"Inside job was it, lads?" Buster puts his hands in his trouser pockets and faces them.

"You've got our money tied up in that pub and I want it back," demands Scott.

"Yeah, we want it back," echoes Greg slapping his wrench in the palm of his hand

"Do you intend using those?" asks Buster, not in the least bit afraid.

Carl looks at his wrench and appears embarrassed.

"Oh, no. My battery cable's loose on the van again. We were just trying to fix it before you came home and I..."

"Shut up!" snaps Scott. "I want in on the pub. I want a share in the profits, which are quite tidy from what I hear."

"Oh, yeah? Help yourself," says Buster. He turns and walks towards his front door.

"Playing the tough guy now?"

Buster and Dwayne stop by their door and turn to face them.

"No. We just don't own the pub any more, as of an hour ago. All sold."

"Hostel takeover, I think they call it," says Dwayne, dejected.

"Does that mean we don't have jobs now?" asks Carl.

"Yup."

"Oh, man!"

"So, if you sold it, you must have the money to pay us back then," says Scott.

"Nope. Don't have any," replies Buster.

"You trying to tell me that you sold a pub with half a million dollars of stolen money and don't have a dime to show for it?" asks Scott.

"Pretty much. Blame the economy."

"And I'm supposed to believe you?" asks Scott.

"I don't care what you believe. We've got nothin', so you've got nothin'."

"We've got three against two, that's what we've got." Scott takes a step towards them.

Just then, Tiffany's apartment door opens and out step three scruffy, disheveled-looking homeless men.

Greg rears backwards.

"Scott! They've got Zombies!"

Tiffany and Rachel emerge from behind the homeless trio.

"Oh, hello, boys," Tiffany says. "What are you doing back this early? I was going to walk Rachel and her friends to the library. Good, now we can take the car." She spots Carl and Greg. "Hello, how are you, boys?" Tiffany walks up to Carl and gives him a big hug.

"Not too shabby, thanks for asking," Carl says. Scott looks bemused. "This is Scott, our…friend."

"Hello. I'm Tiffany, Buster's girlfriend. And this is my daughter, Rachel."

"You're the Ron's Supermarket manager," says Rachel.

"That's right."

"You should put children's cereals and foods at a child's eye level, not up where only the parents can see them. You'll make more money if the child is the one that picks up the product."

Scott is rather impressed.

"Never thought about that, thanks."

"Anybody want a cup of tea?" asks Tiffany.

"No, thanks. I get acid reflux," says Greg. "I'd kill for a glass of milk, though."

"Boys. We're here to do business," says Scott, trying to be cryptic in front of those who do not know their story. "So, Mr. Wide, I look forward to concluding this matter with you in the very near future."

"Over a beer, perhaps?" says Buster, sarcastically.

Scott, Carl and Greg turn and walk down the stairs.

Tiffany tilts her head to one side, thoughtfully.

"Who's running the Tilting Tavern if Carl and Greg aren't there and neither are you two?"

"Let's go back inside and we'll tell you everything," says Buster.

That evening, Buster, Tiffany and Rachel join Dwayne and Aurora at their apartment. The smell of incense competes with the aromatic candles. Bamboo curtains are drawn closed and from the speakers come the sounds of waves crashing on a beach and seagulls squawking.

Dwayne stands between the two large houseplants singing *The Lion Sleeps Tonight* in a very bad, high-pitched voice. He is holding the rabbit and moving it around in a playful manner in front of Rachel who is doing the same with the tortoise.

Aurora sits on her yoga mat in the lotus position. Before her, sit the three homeless men still in their ragged and dirty clothing.

"So that's really what *The Shhh* is all about; channeling positive energy to propel your affluence in a forward direction," she lectures. "Now we're going to do some past-life explorations to see what you did back then that has led you to be homeless in this one. After that, we're going to do a little Reiki healing and Tarot card reading, which is normally a seventy-nine dollar session."

Buster and Tiffany lie side by side on beanbags, watching Dwayne sing and play with Rachel and the animals. Buster pulls Tiffany in closer and hugs her.

"Don't worry, luv, I got it all under control," he assures her. "Oh, I don't suppose you got to see the lotto numbers, did you?"

"Yeah."

"And?"

"You didn't get one single number right," says Tiffany.

"Again."

"Yes," says Buster with glee, clenching a fist in victory. "Another five bucks not wasted."

"I know you're trying your best, Buster, but a lucky break would be useful right now."

"It will come, in the form of silly money from sillier people."

"You mean the potato chip thing?"

"Yup." Buster turns to his brother. "Hey Dwayne, what were the auction prices at the last time you looked?"

Dwayne stops singing and thinks.

"Elvis was at three grand and the Pope was at almost seven grand. The others will fetch a little, but those are our front-runners."

"See?" Buster says reassuringly to Tiffany. "Ten grand on two chips. Probably more when all our auctions end tomorrow. And we only spent about sixty bucks on packets. Could have been half that if we hadn't bought packets of Pringles. Live and learn."

"And gained three pounds by eating the bad ones," adds Dwayne, handing the bunny off to Rachel and emerging from the foliage.

"We need a regular income that we can rely on, other than mine," says Tiffany.

"Well, that gallery owner in Beverly Hills finally got back to me after all this time and wants to see more work by the artist. Said somethin' about puttin' on an art show on Rodeo Drive just for her work, if they can authenticate the artist, whatever that means." He looks to Rachel. "You up for more paintin', Rachel?"

"Sure, as long as I get my cut of the proceeds. I want to start my pension portfolio."

"You're nine."

"Yeah, I should have started last year, but it's never too late," she says.

"Can we have a little less talking, please?" says Aurora, impatiently. "We're regressing into our past lives and we can't hear ourselves think back then."

Even before finishing his first cup of morning coffee, Scott is sitting in his office at the Ron's Supermarket, with not so much a heavy load on his mind as on his lap. A very curvaceous, young female register clerk plays with his hair as he strokes her leg.

At the sound of someone knocking on the door, Scott pushes the girl off his lap and tidies his hair. He snaps his fingers at the clerk, who scurries to the other side of the desk and sits in a chair, as though nothing were amiss.

"Yes?" calls out Scott. The door opens. Lawanda, the supervisor, stands in the doorway. "So, next time that happens, you're to go straight to Lawanda here, okay?" says Scott to the young clerk.

"Yes, Mr. Linus. Sorry, Mr. Linus." She gets up and walks past the supervisor on her way out of the office.

"Yes?" asks Scott, unaware of the smudge of lipstick on his cheek.

Lawanda eyes the lipstick suspiciously before returning to the reason for her interruption.

"Mr. Linus, I think you'll want to meet these two people. They say they've found the stolen money."

Scott looks shocked.

"They've what? Who has?"

Buster and Dwayne appear in the doorway, with big grins on their faces. Buster is holding a bag.

Later that afternoon, Buster, Dwayne and Tiffany gather around the computer screen in Tiffany's apartment examining the final bids on their chips on eBay.

"Just a minute to go on the Pope," calls out Tiffany, excited.

"Thirteen thousand, eight hundred and seventy five dollars just for the Pope!" exclaims Buster. "I knew there was money in the religion racket, but not like this. We could do a whole franchise; Jesus, the Virgin Mary, even the Son, the Father and Holy Ghost."

"That's one person," explains Tiffany.

"Oh. How's Elvis doin'?"

Dwayne clicks over to another bid that has a little longer to go.

"Presley is at seven thousand four hundred and ten, while Costello is only at two thousand three hundred."

"That's probably because Elvis Costello's still alive," remarks Tiffany.

"Pity," mutters Buster. "How's the Maggie Thatcher one coming on?"

Dwayne clicks over to another eBay page and scrolls down to the auction.

"A buck, thirty-eight."

"My friend at the homeless shelter said it looked more like Cliff Richard, if you turned it upside down," says Tiffany. They all contort themselves to look at the image upside down.

"Oh, yeah," marvels Dwayne.

"What's the difference between Maggie Thatcher and Cliff Richard then?" asks Tiffany.

"One is old, shriveled and wrinkly, and the other used to be our Prime Minister," explains Buster. "Back to the Pope, then."

Dwayne clicks back to the page with the Pope potato chip bids. The price seems to be going up and up as the seconds tick away.

"Holy moly," mutters Tiffany. "Fourteen grand now."

"Twenty seconds to go," says Dwayne.

"Fourteen and three hundred."

"Fourteen four."

"Five seconds."

"Fourteen five."

"Fourteen five fifty," shrieks Tiffany.

"Time!" exclaims Dwayne. They all lean in to look at the final amount.

"Fourteen thousand six hundred and twenty five dollars," calls out Dwayne.

"Whoooo-hoooooo!" hollers Buster, as he high-fives his brother and kisses Tiffany. "Wow, that's amazing! Keep an eye on the others and I'll fetch the chips. And make sure to get the lunatic bidder's address so we can send it to him before he changes his mind."

In the bedroom, an elated Buster bursts in to find one of Tiffany's homeless charges sitting on their bed, reading a book, while eating the special chips out of the bowl. Buster stares with disbelief at the homeless man, who has flakes of chips in his wiry beard.

"Did you want one? There were only a few in here," he says, tilting the empty bowl towards Buster.

Buster stares unblinking at the bowl and lets out a whimper.

Mr. Patton sits at his desk in his corner office. Floor-to-ceiling windows on two sides reveal the panoramic vistas of Santa Barbara. His large desk appears diminutive in the very spacious office and he looks even more diminutive behind the large desk. The walls are adorned with awards in the shapes of pub beer levers and oversized beer mats. Interspersed with the awards are photographs of Patton with distinguished celebrities.

"Yes?" Patton says in response to a knock at the door.

He looks up from some paper to see his secretary in the doorway. She walks in with some difficulty, owing to her high-heels and restrictive skirt.

"You know that wonky bar you bought for next to nothing?"

"Of course."

"Look at this," she says, placing some papers before him. "These are from the building permit office."

Patton raises his eyebrows, wrinkling his forehead causing his glasses to slip from the top of his forehead to the bridge of his nose.

"These are permit rejections we were unaware of at the time of purchase."

"Permit rejections?" Patton flips the pages, growing angry.

"That's not all. The money that was stolen from our Calabasas store was returned today."

"Really?" Patton looks up, the good news taking the edge off the permit problem.

"Funny thing is," continues the secretary, "the two people who found the money are the same people you bought the pub from, Buster and Dwayne Wide. The media are all over it."

Mr. Patton puts down the papers.

"Well, well, well. How very coincidental," he says.

"And they asked about a reward."

"Oh, they did, did they?"

# CHAPTER 8

The sun cooks the asphalt of the parking lot outside Ron's Supermarket in Calabasas. Three local television news trucks, with tall antennae protruding from their roofs, are parked near the front entrance.

Inside, shoppers go about their business, occasionally stealing glances at the cluster of people who have gathered in the produce section for a special presentation. The small crowd consists of friends, family, members of the press and some of Ron's staff members. Also lurking is the youth who stole the pink bike and Michael who is signing autographs for people who think he is someone famous. At the front of the gathering, near Rachel and Tiffany, are the three TV reporters with blindingly white teeth, sharp suits and smooth voices, each of whom is shadowed by a less fashion-conscious cameraman. At the back of the crowd stand a curious Carl and Greg.

Disinterested in the news conference happening nearby, Aurora examines the quality of the vegetables in a different part of the produce section. She leans in to get a better look at the beets when the sprinkler misting system kicks in, spraying her face. She steps back, annoyed, looks around to see if anyone was watching, then briskly walks away.

Behind a microphone, stand Mr. Patton, his secretary, Scott Linus, his supervisor Lawanda and the smartly-dressed Wide brothers. Scott looks at his watch, ready to start the proceedings. He rearranges the knot on his tie, conscious of the TV cameras, then steps up to the microphone.

"Ladies and... lemen. I'd like... welco...you all... the... arket. We here at... are....ppy to ..." Scott smiles and taps the microphone. "Ha. Nothing wrong with the microphone. Just my little joke, breaks the ice at parties, you know." Nobody even

93

cracks a smile. Mr. Patton stares at him with disdain. Scott clears his throat. "Anyway. We're gathered here today to thank two very interesting people, Buster and Dwayne Wide. These gentlemen are better known to the public as the owners of the Tilting Tavern, which apparently we now own." He looks back at Mr. Patton. "Although nobody tells me anything," he mutters. "So, with no further ado, let me give you the CFO of Brenton Brewery, Mr. Chuck Patton, who will present a commemorative plaque thanking our most ethical and morally responsible citizens for returning the stolen money, that they *allegedly* found in the middle of nowhere."

Cameras flash. Scott steps to one side, allowing Mr. Patton to approach the microphone to light applause.

"Thank you, Mr. Linus. So good to see you back with us after an extended leave due to post traumatic heist disorder." He smiles condescendingly at Scott who hams it up for the cameras. "As CFO of Brenton Brewery I am grateful, make that honored, to be here to accept the return of the stolen money that these two fine upstanding citizens..."

"Er, green card holders," corrects Dwayne, leaning forward into the mic. "We ain't citizens yet, just got green cards."

"That these fine *green card* holders managed to somehow find at the side of the road," continues Mr. Patton, as he glances to Buster and Dwayne. "From the bottom of my heart and from all the shareholders of Brenton Brewery, I'd just like to say a hearty..."

"Clean up on aisle three, clean up on aisle three," interjects a voice over the speaker system.

Annoyed, Mr. Patton clears his throat before continuing:

"...a hearty thank you. We are here to recognize your honest and moral action in returning this money to us." There is loud applause, which then dies down. "How did you manage to find the money, anyway?"

Dwayne steps up to the microphone.

"Shhh!" he whispers.

"It's a secret?" asks Mr. Patton.

"No, that's how we found it. By the power of *The Shhh*."

Scott quickly steps up to the microphone.

"*The Shhh* DVD on sale at the checkout for only twelve ninety-nine. Two for twenty-five. Grab them while stocks last." He steps back.

A bewildered Mr. Patton steps up to the microphone again.

"It gives me a modicum of pleasure to present this plaque of thanks for returning the money to Ron's Supermarket, to Buster and Dwayne Wide."

There is a loud round of applause as the brothers step up to the microphone. His secretary hands Mr. Patton a rather pathetic plaque about the size of a salad plate. Mr. Patton then hands it to Buster and Dwayne. Handshakes ensue all around as cameras flash and TV lenses zoom in on the proceedings.

Rachel hands Tiffany a tissue, as her mother tears up.

Buster smiles at the cameras and leans into the microphone.

"Thank you, thank you. Ladies, gentlemen and extinguished guests. We're happy to accept this great honor. We see it as just doin' our duty. I mean, we could easily have kept it. After all, it was just lying there on the ground – half a million bucks, just lying there – doin' nothin', unwanted – looking for a home," says Buster, staring into space, his voice trailing off with a hint of remorse. "But, no, we did the right thing and here we are now receivin' this honor for it."

Mr. Patton leans in to the microphone.

"Are there any questions from the press?"

There is a flurry of questions. Buster points to the same female reporter that interviewed him and Dwayne outside the pub.

"Hello, Mandy. How are ya, luv?" asks Buster.

"Fine, thanks. Exactly how did you find the money, Mr. Wide?"

"We had to pull over to the side of the road when the car was overheatin'. Dwayne went to take a toilet break and that's when he saw the bag just lying there in the grass."

"I sensed it was there as I visualized the presence of abundance," adds Dwayne, leaning into the microphone.

Aurora looks up from examining the cauliflowers and gives Dwayne a wry smile of approval.

"As soon as my brother came back with the bag, I knew it was probably the money stolen in the supermarket robbery," explains Buster. "So I – we – felt it our civil duty to return it to its rightful owner."

"I bet you did," mutters a bitter Scott.

"Were you at all tempted to keep the money and not tell anyone?" asks another reporter.

"Well, yeah, but..." starts Dwayne.

"No, no. Not at all," interjects Buster with a fake smile. "As soon as we saw it lying there we knew we had to return it to its rightful owners, so we could collect the reward."

"What reward might that be?" asks Mr. Patton.

"The fifty big ones for returning the money," he says, holding the smile for the cameras.

"Oh, no, there's no reward," says Mr. Patton. "If there was, it would be for the capture and conviction of the robbers and not for the return of the money. That's what the plaque is for." Now Mr. Patton wears the smile of victory.

"Do what?" Buster struggles to hold his fake smile.

Scott leans into the microphone, also basking in the shallow victory of revenge.

"Unless you know the identity of the robbers, Mr. Wide?" He looks out into the crowd. "And how on earth could you possibly know that?"

In the crowd, Carl and Greg hide their faces, then gingerly retreat.

"No reward?" The smile on Buster's face is faltering.

"Nope, zip, naught, nada, nothing, big...fat...zero!" says Scott, chin up, looking down his nose at Buster.

Mr. Patton pats Buster on the shoulder.

"Just the satisfaction in knowing that you have done the right thing. And who can put a price on that, eh?" he says.

Heads hung low, Buster and Dwayne saunter with Aurora, Tiffany and Rachel towards their car in the supermarket parking lot. Dwayne looks at the plaque.

"So, do we keep it six months each or each have it for a month at a time?" he asks. Buster shoots him a look of disdain.

"Never mind, love," soothes Aurora. "I'll make you a tofu-vegetable wrap with bean sprouts and bee pollen. Then, after a colonic, we'll de-stress with meditation."

Dwayne stops short.

"I don't want your bloody tofu bee pollen sprouted rabbit food, *Janet*!" he says defiantly in a loud voice. "I want a burger and fries and, damn it, I'm going to have burger and fries if I want to."

Aurora folds her arms, unimpressed.

"Dwayne."

"What?"

"Starve the anger, feed the love. Now get in the car."

"Yes, dear." Dwayne sheepishly does as Aurora says.

"I see, cars are bad things unless you have to walk or get the bus home, is that it?" says Buster.

"You're already burning fossil fuels, so why not make the most of it?" Aurora smiles condescendingly and climbs in the back of the Ford.

Buster stands by his open car door as Rachel squeezes into the back seat.

"Now what do we do?" asks Tiffany. "The chip thing went belly-up and you were counting on that reward to see us through."

"Yeah, I know." Buster thinks, then looks across the parking lot and sees Carl and Greg about to get into their 1976 VW van.

"Oy, Carl!" shouts out Buster. "Hang on a sec."

The flamboyant Rodeo Drive art gallery manager sits at his desk across from Buster, who is still wearing the suit from his recent supermarket appearance.

"Although the art is very appealing, and in vogue right now, we're not totally satisfied with its authenticity. We performed our due diligence and couldn't find anything on the artist at all. There's no such artist that we can find anywhere."

"Oh, yes there is. You wanna meet her?" asks Buster with a wry smile.

"Sure."

Buster steps to one side and Carl appears in the doorway wearing the same dress, wig and makeup he wore to pull off the supermarket robbery.

"Hi," he says with bashful wave.

"That's her?" the manager asks, clearly surprised.

"In the flesh. Although there's a little more of it, if you know what I mean?"

The manager is now quite excited.

"Oh, yes, transgender artists are in high demand in Beverly Hills right now." He steps out from behind his desk.

"It is?" says Buster amazed. "Oh, yeah, of course it is."

The manager eagerly walks up to Carl and turns him around, looking him up and down. Carl feels like a prize Heifer at the auction.

"Personal appearances will certainly help sales. Especially if the artist is a looker like this one. Let's discuss over a half-caff, soy frappachino, shall we?"

He leads a wide-eyed Carl out of the office, leaving Buster to smile to himself.

Meanwhile, Dwayne is trying his hand at busking in the Calabasas mall. Busking is a very liberal term associated with what Dwayne is actually doing. He has brushed off the cobwebs from his plastic leather, Vegas-style outfit with fake pot-belly extension, donned his bald skullcap with grey horse-shoe of hair and bushy sideburns, and stepped into a pair of gaudy platform shoes in order to perform his "If-Elvis-were-alive-today" routine. He steps up to a cheap microphone that leads into a battery-powered amplifier and speakers and sings to the tune of a 50's rock and roll background track:

*"I was the King of Rock and Roll, I was rich as Croesus.*
*But now I'm eighty-five and falling to pieces.*
*Living in a home, I ain't feeling complacent.*
*Got my trusty false teeth and a new hip replacement.*
*I still got it…*
*Just look at these moves*
*I still rock it…*
*Although I ain't in the news.*
*I still sock it…*
*Baby, I'm in the groove*
*I still bop it…*
*In my orthopedic shoes."*

Dwayne channels the spirit of a geriatric Elvis Presley, gyrating his hips and making a spectacle of himself. It is not easy to tell if the onlookers are impressed or mortified by his routine.

*"I used to have hair that was wavy and high*
*Now I've got hair that's waving goodbye!*
*I was gorgeous and trim with a tight little butt*
*Now I got arthritis and a purulent gut.*
*I still shake it ...*
*Like I used to do*
*I still fake it ...*
*Like I did my King Fu*
*I medicate it ...*
*With the pills that are blue*
*I still make it ...*
*Except to the loo."*

As Dwayne continues to gyrate, a woman in the crowd is clearly moved by his performance and wipes tears from her eyes.

"I just love Roy Orbison," she says.

That evening, the mood at Tiffany's apartment is somber. Rachel sits on the living room floor with one of the homeless men, going over a quantum physics book and making notes. Tiffany sits in a chair having her hair cut by a homeless woman. The television plays the end credits of a reality show.

Buster, in casual clothes, slouches against the sofa's armrest with several packets of crisps around his legs and on the floor. He examines each one, holding it up against the light to see if it bears any resemblance to someone famous. On the carpet by him is an empty bowl signifying that he has not had any luck so far.

"So, we've talked about spin operators and commutation relationships," says the homeless man to Rachel. "Now we should move on to the Hamiltonian, the Heisenberg Uncertainty Principle and the Schrödinger Equation."

"In relation to the Compton Effect?" asks Rachel.

"Exactly," says the homeless man.

Buster holds up a chip.

"Think this looks anything like Marilyn Monroe?" he asks.

Rachel looks up from her books and leans in closer.

"More like Marilyn Manson."

"Oh," says Buster. Disappointed, he puts the chip in his mouth and bites down on it.

"Who's probably more famous than Monroe these days," she adds.

Buster stops chewing.

"How?" he asks through a mouthful of chip crumbs.

"He's a Goth singer. Cult following."

Buster spits out the pieces of the now chewed chip to see if he can salvage it.

On the TV, the credits end and the lottery result segment begins. There is little introductory music, just a groomed man in a suit with a plastic smile standing next to the clear container, where numerous white balls are being bounced around by jets of air.

"Good evening, ladies and gentlemen. Welcome to tonight's much anticipated lottery draw, as the jackpot rollover is two hundred and sixty million dollars." The camera is tight in on the bouncing balls as they are randomly chosen. "First one out, number seven, number seven."

Buster glances up but takes no real notice. He finds another chip and examines it.

"You've got split ends," comments the homeless woman cutting Tiffany's hair. "You have the type of hair that should air-dry only. The heat from the blow dryer is making your hair brittle."

"Number forty-four, number forty-four," calls out the announcer.

"So, you're saying that the angular momentum of an electron bound to an atom or molecule is quantized?" asks Rachel, looking at the homeless man.

"Only in the context of quantum mechanics do the wave-particles duality of energy and matter and the uncertainty principle provide a unified view of the behavior of photons, electrons and other sub-atomic-scale objects."

"Number sixteen, sixteen," calls out the television presenter.

Tiffany looks over to Buster.

"Aren't those your usual numbers?" she asks. "If you bothered playing, that is."

"Yeah." Buster holds up a chip. "This looks like an otter. D'you think animals will fetch much on eBay?"

"Number three, that's number three."

"That's four now!" exclaims Tiffany, politely raising a hand to stop the woman working on her hair.

Now the program has Buster's attention. He looks to the
television and watches as the blowing machine spins and tumbles
the remaining balls.

"And the fifth ball is…" Another ball is sucked from the
laundry of spinning balls. "Forty-five, that's forty five."

Buster sits up abruptly, leaning forward, staring at the TV with
mouth agape.

"That's everything but the mega ball isn't it, Buster?" asks
Tiffany, staring intently at the TV. "Don't you have number nine
as the mega number?"

"Shh!"

"And now, for that all-important mega ball." The balls bounce
around before the last one is sucked out.

"Number nine. The mega ball is number nine."

Tiffany stares at the screen, unable to move.

Buster also stares at the television, dumbfounded at what has
just happened. He holds his breath for a long time, absorbing the
ramifications, then lets it out with an almost inaudible whimper.


## THE END